Wilderness

of

Literacy

Hypocrisy & Reality

Book:2

fiction
by
'Videh' Arvind Kumar

1962 to 1964
(a novel)
(informal: classes 1st to 3rd)
(Maar-Haraa, Jhaajhar,
Kunwarpur, Jaabil)

Dedication
Wilderness of Literacy
(Hypocrisy & Reality:
Book 2)

Dedicated to my extremely affectionate mother who initiated me into the wonderland of literacy and who was a constant source of support for me throughout my struggles in the days of schooling!

Table of Contents

Copyright

Preface

'Wilderness of Literacy' is the second volume in the long fiction series 'Hypocrisy & Reality' and, as the name suggests, it takes the protagonist in the arena of letters, words, and numbers: the realm of what we call the 'literacy'. The experience of a child while treading this seemingly dreaded as well as untrodden landscape is nothing short of venturing into a wilderness; of course, led and mentored first by one's parents and thereafter invariably by their preceptors -- the masters -- all of whom have a tremendous amount of impact on the future human being that emerges from their inputs given and endeavours made towards making a man, the humanity.

'Videh' Arvind Kumar
Aashrum, Lucknow, UP, India
July, 2024

Transcripts of *Hindee* letters and *maatraas*

Keeping in view the special pronunciations of *Sanskrit* words, and with a view to differentiating between the disparate pronunciations, we have followed the following regimen of transcription from *Devnaagaree* to Roman script. This clarification will help the readers appreciate the nuances of linguistic specificities and enjoy the text in truly desired sense. Moreover, the vernacular words, particularly nouns, have been italicized.

अ a, आ aa, इ i, ई ee, उ u, ऊ oo, ऋ ri, ए e, ऐ ai, ओ o, औ ऑ au, अं an, अ: :,
क ka, का kaa, कि ki, की kee, कु ku, कू koo, कृ kri, के ke, कै kai, को ko, कौ kau, कं kan, क: kah;

1. My Mother Initiates Me Into The Wonderland Of Letters

Enter Protagonist

Heretofore, I have been writing. Writing about the reminiscences from the domain where the phenomena of time and space were immaterial, or absent from the scene. Still the protagonist has been able to collate them: how? By virtue of letters, and words, and sentences, and paragraphs, and chapters, *et al*. An abstract phenomenon – the voice, God's gift - - has been transcribed into a sensible as well as communicable material composed of queer signs, symbols and designs. I have been writing in English for the consideration that the same is the language mostly in vogue in present epoch. I can write in one more script, that is, *Devanaagaree* in *Hindee* ; and some amount of *Sanskrit* may also do.

But who was he or she who equipped me with this faculty that is called literacy, and through the instrumentality of which, I am able to create this intriguing saga of truth and reality, and of the life lived by me during this span of time: on this planet.

She was my mother: an illiterate lady! An unlettered persona!

Hailing as I did from a nondescript, rustic hamlet, the only initiating book or booklet available at that time in our village was a tiny six-pager containing *Hindee varnamaalaa* (alphabet) which contained *swar* (vowels) and *vyanjan* (consonants) both, along with their defining pictorial symbols e.g. *A* for *Anaar* or *Ka* for *Kabootar et al.* This booklet was available at the sole grocer's shop of our village, and cost hardly a pie, or almost nothing. Naturally, I was purchased this lean booklet by my mother – not by father – as the latter was an inconsiderate and indifferent father by that time, as my impression of him goes.

I have a hunch that at the time I was initiated into the realm of literacy by my mother, she was at least what may be called 'lettered', if not literate or educated: she could decipher the letters with the help of pictorial symbols from the booklet. For, she uttered to me *A* for *Anaar* (pomegranate), *Ka* for *Kabootar* (pigeon) *et al*; and commanded me to emulate her voice and speak myself after her. She also bought me a wooden *patti* (plaque) and blackened it with carbon powder taken from the back of the black pan; and she used to write *kitkinnaa* (letters to be traced) on the plaque; and then she held my hand affectionately, dipped the reed quill in the white liquid of calcium or chalk, and thus helped me trace the *kitkinnaa* on the plaque. She took great pleasure in lettering me, as I can recollect even at this distance in time. She reposed great hope in me. I feel, I was a sharp child prodigy at that time also, and my mother felt glad and proud to see that I had learned the letters quite quickly, and also, that I was able to trace the *kitkinnaa,* of my own: without the hand-holding by my mother. Mother was very young at that age: definitely in her twenties and was a beauty, a lovely and affectionate face, to be proud of.

Then there were other family lads and lasses, too, who took charge of lettering me, of their own volition; and I have a vivid memory of their appreciation for my extraordinary gifts in learning the language, that is, alphabet. When they expressed amazement at my innate gift of linguistic sharpness, I felt myself amused to think why they were so much surprised at this natural correctness of learning the letters on my part. They used to comment by and by that I would have been a highly intellectual person in my previous birth, to my bewilderment and astonishment.

Nonetheless, when I recall those incidents which verged on utter obscenity as well as incivility on my childish part I feign pretend to be an intellectual soul in my previous birth. Rather, I am constrained to think that I would have been a *Yaksha* in any one of my innumerable previous births. Such incidents were not far and few between, rather, those were uncomfortably frequent in number. For instance, whenever I was faced with a situation of strife, that is, fight against some rival – of course, of my child age – and I would find myself unequal to the rival's strength and prowess, I would invariably resort to abusive language and would start abusing him in the most obscene and foul tongue, even implying the raping of the opponent's mother and sister; why only that, even fucking him. And amusingly, the implements or organs that I would suggest to be used for doing so would be my own procreational organs. So despicable indeed! But childish by all manners! Nevertheless, even in that state of charged atmosphere of rage I could feel palpably in my heart that I was doing something utterly wrong and objectionable. Then I wondered why it was that despite my inner voice objecting to my using that sort of foul language I was not finding myself up to restraining myself then and there. I also wondered even at that moment as to who might be there inside me other than my conscious self before whom I was feeling so helpless! This realisation would be so palpable that I used to repent after having indulged in those ugly scenes and having done those fouls in societal norms of civility.

Let's take an instance. It so happened the other day during the festival of *Holee* – the festival of colours meant, in turn, to celebrate the harvest season in Spring – that someone soiled and spoiled my dress by throwing the dirty mud taken from the street puddle. I being a child took it as an affront to my childlike dignity. As a result, I rushed to the roof of my thatched *kutcha* room and from there peaking onto the street where the hoodlums of children – the *Holee* revellers – were wallowing in the street puddles composed of night soil and urinated waters, I started off addressing them in the foulest abusive tongue as delineated here-in-above. And that harangue continued for several minutes, and in the most fervent childish manner! To the amusement and bemusement of the bystanders – the revellers – in the street. They did not mind, however, whatever I was barking; for they themselves were using the similar sort of abusive lexicon all along, most of them being dead drunk.

My elder aunt – *Taaee* – of course, who was there in the house down below was taking cognizance of what I was barking, but she was incapable of climbing the roof where I was perched and barking, because there were no ladders or stairs to reach the roof. In none of the village dwelling units there used to be any staircases, as a matter of fact; and whenever there arose a need for reaching the roof – for instance, for repair *et al* – ladders made of bamboo poles were used. Fortunately for me, there was no bamboo ladder available readily for the *Taaee* at that moment; and I could thus be safe as regards summary punishment – the

beating -- by my aunt. Amazingly, I had no risk of being punished by my own mother; she seldom reprimanded me for my abusive behaviour or for my foul tongue. She rather, out of her love for her only son, would think that all that was merely a childish tantrum. My aunt nonetheless opted to shout at me from below in a sarcastic as well as loud tone, "*Shaabaash!*" (Bravo! Well done!) Seeing her facial expression and the tone, despite being a child, I could immediately make out that she was up for something dangerous towards me. I was instead hoping that my elders would be glad to see the spectacular bravado their progeny was displaying so brazenly in front of the melee in the street, that is, before the entire village community. It was rather just the converse! They were ashamed that their progenies were so ill-mannered and that fact was being laid bare in front of the entire village!

I then feared my immediate fate post that incident and I climbed down from the roof towards the opposite direction of my aunt, that is, towards the back side of the house; in fact the wall or roof on that side was not that high, and I could jump down safely onto the dust or mud dumped there around. To ensure that I should escape punishment from my elder aunt, I relied on the faculty of forgetfulness of the grown-ups, and to reach that stage – of onset of forgetfulness – I whiled away time playing with the children away from the harm's way till late in the evening.

Nothing happened when I returned home in the evening, as if nothing was the matter at all; my aunt was busy with more serious rigmaroles of her life as usual than those trivialities.

However, that was not a one off instance; such episodes were quite frequent, rather, were the norm as far as I was concerned. That is why I am tempted to deduce that I would have been a *Yaksha* in one of my previous births long back in antiquity. And that deep *sanskaar* of *Yakshatva* would raise its hood now and then, to my utter helplessness. That helplessness also suggested to me that there was no 'I' within me, which I surmised as my 'self', rather, it was all an ensemble of *Sanskaars* and the resultant *'Vigyaan'* leading, in turn, to my compulsive actions.

Not that the habit of using abusive foul language persisted only during my babyhood or childhood, that habit persisted throughout my life. That's why I strongly feel that I would have been an erstwhile *Yaksha* in anyone of my previous births.

But why should I have developed or picked up that despicable habit of using foul language in my babyhood or childhood should be discerned in scientific modern terms as well, the theory of *Yakshatva* in previous birth

notwithstanding. The reason was that there was an atmosphere of *Yakshatva* prevalent all around in that society itself and at that juncture itself; and the first input came from my own father at home where he would be a daily nuisance for my mother and other inhabitants; where he would invariably be creating ruckus and using most obscene language that I used in turn. Outside the house, too, every person without exception used the similar type of lexicon whenever one found oneself in the state of rage or helplessness against someone else, or especially, against the helpless poor subservient strata of society. They were all casteist feudal folks who believed in tyranny and had no regard for or idea about what was called the *dhaammik* living. Moreover, they used those foul terms without meaning them; that is, they never thought that the terms they were using were utterly objectionable insofar as they would use the term 'fuck your sister' against their own son and in the very presence of their daughter herself, and without any remorse or qualms of conscience.

Another similar despicable trait was the 'ingratitude', the lack of feeling grateful towards the benefactors. I seldom felt obliged to those who did something good for me or helped me during my dire straits. It was only later in life that I realised that this trait of being ungrateful was a very pernicious *sanskaar* in human life, having very grave consequences for future life and births. However, to be true, I felt that I had inculcated that habit possibly from my mother who seldom showed genuine sense of gratitude towards whoever showed her the generosity of heart or mind, or whoever helped her in her moments of urgency or emergency.

Having said all that, I intend to vouch that despite being mentally sharp and drawing profuse praise from my elders both at home, family and school, I was not such a gem as regards basic human virtues; I was a foul-mouthed child, an ungrateful child, and also, one that indulged in childish self-sex fondling with my sex organ.

XXX

2. Illiteracy: The Fallout Of Helping My Sibling Survive

Enter Mother

This is not that I was any less efficient or less intelligent that I could not pursue my studies or could not make myself worthy of being counted among literates, or that I was not interested in going to school or reading. I was equally zealous to go to school, and I did start going to school in the primitive standards, too, in the nearby village of ours.

However, as the fate would have it, the ill luck struck me indirectly through the calamity that stalked my elder sister – *Gyaan*, or *Gyaano*, as we called her. She was married at not-so-distant a village from ours, on the side-lines of a railroad, on the way to our nearest city. In her prime, at her in-laws' abode, once while white-washing her *kutcha* thatched dwelling with liquid lime, a droplet of liquid lime got into her eye inadvertently: and all hell broke loose! It was a grave mishap: a pretty young lady getting defaced with one eye going out of shape, looking odd. All out efforts were made clinically as well as medically to restore the original beauty of the eye and the eyesight, but to no avail.

Incidentally, she had only a few days back, too, been struck by yet another tragedy in the manner of death of his only son – quite a youth. She and her husband were shattered totally at that juncture in their lives.

To help them run the household and to add some sense of sanguinity in their daily chores, I as an adolescent girl – her younger sister -- was deputed to her village in that moment of their grave calamity. The help I could provide although, the new friends I could make there though – like that with *Saavitree* – but my education got sacrificed in the process, the goddess of literacy – the *Saraswatee* – forsook me. The time as usual passed at its normal pace, and bypassed me eventually in the process. Nonetheless, the girls remaining uneducated or illiterate was not a big incident or deal those days; the education of girls was not a compulsory attribute, the lack of which should have been bemoaned; rather, the lesser literate a girl, the better, seemed to be the notion prevalent in those days in Indian milieu! I craved education and schooling, too, but for my hard luck!

Hard luck I have had all along ever since. I was married with a most qualified husband in the area, yet all his education proved naught as regards his worthiness for leading a normal if only not a respectable life. My life as well as education was thus sacrificed for the sake of my elder sister!

XXX

3. (Guileless Phool*!*

Enter Mausaajee *(Husband of Sister of my Mother)*

Phool's stay at our village was a pleasurable memory in our lifetime. She was an adolescent blonde at that juncture of her age. However, she was a shy girl as becoming of all pretty blondes. Her shyness and guilelessness could be testified by following episode: one late morning, I along with one of my friends was sitting on my *chaarpoy* smoking *hukkaa* at our *chaupaal*. I sighted adolescent *Phool* standing amongst the buffaloes, sort of struggling all alone, on her own. I thought, it was some trifling issue. Nonetheless, after a while, I heard

her summon me for rescue and there was desperation in her voice, "*Jeejaa*, this buffalo is recalcitrant; she is not budging!" The awkwardness of communication and ambiguity of meaning contrived to confuse me all the more, and I could not make out anything of what she had uttered. Once again, she summoned me for assistance, this time shouting, as though wailing, "This buffalo is recalcitrant, she does not heed me." The panic in her voice this time alarmed me and we both rushed towards her. And lo! we found that her tender and pretty feet had been crushed under the hoof of the innocent buffalo – though the poor creature didn't mean any harm intentionally, nor did it know anything about what had eventually been trampled under its hooves. The sufferer was equally innocent, not to know how to summon assistance of humans and how to describe one's predicament when got caught amidst cattle or beasts. She was not saying outright that her foot was getting crushed under the hoof of the hefty buffalo; instead, she was complaining against the disobedience and recalcitrance of the buffalo – a cattle: the caller herself also nothing short of a cattle in that sense! Disobedience on the part of a cattle or a beast is a no-brainer and a non-issue; this needs to be known and must needs to be made known to children.

Furthermore, being a pretty and attractive girl, she was bound to come within the focus of attraction of the youth of her age. It is quite natural: nothing special or bizarre about it! All the girls turn attractive and seductive at a certain age; also, it is true that all the women lose all the charm whatever after a certain age thereafter! It's so ephemeral, everything! So fleeting, so transient! Especially attracted towards her was *Chandra*, the son of my friend as well as neighbour, the brother of *Phool*'s fast friend, *Saavitree*. The boy might be enamoured but the girl was underwhelmed by his overtures and, as a result, she always remained shy at our village whatever the romantic feelings of the lad.

We never saw her talk to *Chandra*, even in her later adult life thereafter, possibly due to this earlier miscarriage of interaction or irritating overtures. The incidents of childhood have their inevitable say in shaping the adult life!

XXX

Table of Contents

4. To The Paathshaalaa Of My Village

Enter Protagonist

May be it was 1961! The exodus of Britishers took place almost 14 years back and the so-called Freedom was trying itself to get established, rooted, so to say. The education was considered as the most valuable input that was required to be imparted to the citizens for turning them into valuable assets for the just freed and fledgling nation, and also, for safeguarding the newly introduced system of Governance called 'Democracy' immediately after decimating the so-far prevalent system of feudalism and princely states. In the euphoria as well as the fog of undefined phenomenon called republic or democracy, everybody was willing zealously to sacrifice whatever one had. And, of course, it was only the regality of approximately 565 states that had all the wealth of the nation accumulated unto themselves. They had eventually to sacrifice their all, their estates as well as states, their rights, their power and authority, and ultimately their wealth and status and, in turn, their dissipated style of living, which was so despised and reviled by all and sundry of the nation who were ruled by them.

Nevertheless, if one set-up was being dismantled, the roots of another equally wily and cunning set-up were being laid: this time by the lawyers instructed in the British legal system. It was the British legal system when imparted to the natives in the shape of educating them that proved self-annihilating as well as suicidal for the Britishers and cost them ultimately their empire, for, in their enthusiasm to educate the colonial subjects, they forgot that the same subjects would use the same education and law – which was meant for civilised and highly cultured clans – for advancing their own selfish interests and would grab the power and set up their own new sets of dynasties as well as family fiefdoms.

However, since old system was being dismantled and the entire structure of the then extant feudalism was crumbling, everything whatever was to be done by these new rulers of India, was intended to be done clandestinely, that is, in the garb and lexicon of 'republic' and 'democracy'. And to give credence to their designs so that nobody suspected their intentions of grabbing power for themselves, they wrote new compendium, new book of governance, and called that as 'Constitution'. Earlier, in the olden Indian system, the same book was called 'Smriti', which some called as 'Manu Smriti'; now it became *Samvidhaan Smriti*. And though the book was written and supported by a great number of celebrated brains of the time, since the scribe for that book – the chairman of the Drafting Committee -- was *Baabaa Saaheb Ambedkar*, his followers, rather the people of his caste, started calling the book as having been written by him alone, as though solitarily; that is how the history repeats and distorts itself. In prehistoric days, though the *'Jay'* epic, which was later renamed

as *'Bhaarat Yuddha'* and thereafter, as if to aggrandise themselves, to *'Mahaabhaarat Yuddha'*, was supposedly compiled by dozens and more wise men and sages, but the entire credit has gone to the sole sage or author named *'Vyaas'*, who was also supposed to be from a lower caste *a la Ambedkar*. By being a lower caste, one can grab renown more easily: this is true not only in this age, but was true in all the ages gone by, as well.

For everything was to be done and grabbed in the name of republic and democracy, schools were set up throughout the nook and corner of the country, even in the countryside. A school was opened in our village, too. It was christened 'Primary *Paathshaalaa*': a hybrid name of half Anglican and half *Sanskritic* lexicon!

Apart from initiation into the wonderland of letters and *kitkinnaa* by my mother, I was also initiated into the realm of *Paathshaalaa*. And now in hindsight, I can't recollect whether I felt happy and gay at the idea of going to school or not, but I can recollect that it was a novel wonderland, the opening up of a wider spectrum of the world for me, towards the light, the illumination, from the gloom and darkness of ignorance about the other aspects of speech we spoke. The *Paathshaalaa* was there as though to unlock the mystery of speech to me and was there to transcribe the voice into letters and symbols which *per se* looked so crazy. Of course, *Devanaagaree* was our script and the language was called *Hindee* .

The small sized handy book that we had was very easy to carry anywhere; nonetheless, we had a bulky wooden plaque to write on and a small pot full of solution of white chalk or calcium – *Budikkaa* - with which to write, and for the quill, we had soft sticks of reed sharpened in the shape of a quill. Absolute self-sufficiency as regards resources of learning in the interiors of countryside! Yet those primitive resources never seemed to be generating the least of inferiority complex in our child hearts. We were rather glad that everything that was required for getting educated was available locally.

XXX

Enter Protagonist

My initial impression of the adult world was that males were arrogant, vulgar and rustic whereas ladies were affable, civilized and kind-hearted; and the latter seemed to be more sensible than the male members. Male members were always seen with their eyebrows warped. Fortunately, when we were taken to the *Paathshaalaa* of our hamlet, there were all female teachers. We can't guess about their ages but going by the appellations and addresses the people used for them, we can tell now in hindsight that they would have been of young ages. The villagers called them '*Behenjee*' (sisters) and we children, too, called them by that appellation only. *Behenjees* were exceptionally kind towards the kids, or maybe they were obliged to be kind towards the kids, we can't say, for the kids belonged to the who's who of the hamlet and any complaint regarding the mistreatment of children on the part of those young teachers would have invited wrath of the parents invariably.

Nonetheless, the feeling of going to the *Paathshaalaa* was like that of going to some spot for celebration. It felt like a wonderland in a sense. Thus far, we were used to using only the tongue while communicating with other living creatures, like, our mother, father and other related persons and that made sense, that is, the sounds we uttered made some sense: our minds were programmed like that. We had no idea heretofore that the speech we spoke could also be represented in the form of symbols and signs called alphabets and letters; and the numbers we used could be represented likewise in the form of symbols, too; and that the communication could take place even without speaking, and merely by writing on a piece of parchment or on a wooden plaque or on a tiny slab of granite etc. That revelation when made seemed like a wonderland. As though Alice had arrived in Wonderland!

The *Behenjees* hailed not from our hamlet, rather, they were posted here from far off places. They were thus vulnerable as well as shaky, living amidst the savage and rustic villagers. Moreover, the stay arrangements in villages were not available and they had to put up with the households of who's who of the village and, given the social set-up infested with feudal tendencies, there were lot many restrictions on the living of the female folks. It was, in other words, not a life, rather a punishment or a sentence, to be posted to villages. However, all this was being done at the behest of 'Mahaatmaa', the *Gaandhee* , whose own practical knowledge of the Indian social milieu was naught. *Mahaatmaa* didn't know that not everybody who was living in this land was a *Mahaatmaa* like himself. He was no doubt trying to pose as *Mahaatmaa* but in essence he was not one: politically though that garb was suiting him. All his rules and norms were applied to all, except himself; to others, that is. He had never been posted to countryside either, being the scion of a princely state, the son of a Prime Minister of that state.

These *Behenjees* did face the problems like being troubled by the urchins, and even grown-ups, of the village with carnal intents, for sexual pursuits: those lumpens could never think anything else about young ladies or girls except sexual pursuits, savage and rustic as they were. Actually, so far they had been seeing all along that the womenfolk of their village remained veiled and rarely was any young lady seen with her face open and head uncovered like these teachers were. The situation was as bad as some of the shameless lads even hid themselves under the *chaarpoys* of the lady teachers in the school when the latter reached the school to teach the kids. There used to be no chairs available for seating of teachers unlike these days; *chaarpoys* were used for sitting instead, courtesy of someone benevolent in the village. Students, of course, squatted on the jute straps; well, they sat even on the dusty floor before the jute straps were arranged. The teachers made complaints about the foul tongue used by the lumpens and the misdeeds done by them to the elders of the village; but the problem was that the elders themselves were not above-board. After all, the lumpens were the progenies of these savage elders only!

Anyway, we little kids were not much concerned about such social as well as sexual aspects of the schooling arena and about unjustified posting of young girl teachers to the village schools. How they lived, where they ate, how they protected their modesty and chastity amidst these beasts, under what tensions and stresses did they live, was none of our concern. That was *Mahaatmaa*'s concern! He was reported to have been killed long back, yet his soul reigned supreme; entire country was under his spell, as though, after his murder. We were studying, getting lettered, shedding our status of being unlettered, i.e.; the illiteracy!

To support these exotic teachers, there were some elder girls, older than us, who probably studied in upper classes of the school and they helped these teachers in respect of tackling us small kids. We loved those small sisters; they were quite kind and considerate towards me. The reason was that whenever they dictated something to write as regards language I used to write correctly and those sisters expressed surprise at my writing the spellings and *maatraas* correctly. I, in turn, was surprised at their surprise: 'why should I not write correctly?' I could never surmise. The fact of the matter was that all other children wrote incorrectly. My common-sense, however, dictated that I should write like that and it happened to be eventually correct. It had something to do with phonetics. I had subconsciously caught the code of speech and its form in alphabet. That

might be a God gift! Maybe the sisters were right when they attributed this gift to my possibly being a linguistic expert in my previous birth! Who could deny the possibility? I started relishing my divine gift, even as, the teachers started praising my spectacular linguistic skills to one and all and, most of all, to my parents and grandparents.

In *Paathshaalaa*, I had thus assumed the stature of a child prodigy, an extraordinary child scholar! The coming events cast their shadows before, they say! *Honhaar birvaan ke hot cheekne paat!* (The plants that have potential to grow high have their shoots smooth, sound and sturdy!)

XXX

6. *An Unintentional Tiff With A Playmate & Scare Of Hurt*

Enter Protagonist

The days I was studying in *Paathshaalaa*, one of the teachers – lady, of course – resided in the household of one of the brothers of our grandparent. This household was very large, situated at an elevated land, that is, highland, and abounding in dozens of inhabitants. Maybe, the inhabitants had an altruistic tendency as compared to our real grandparent insofar as they offered to help the beleaguered lady – the teacher – whereas our arena was indifferent to the woes of the latter. My observation and empirical inference is that most of the village folks are self-centred and selfish, however different may be the opinion of others – the bookish opinion!

In the same household, one of my classmates – if one would like to call him one – a toddler of my age, of course, was also staying those days; he was actually the son of one of the married girls pertaining to that household. And like me, he had also just started his journey into the wonderland of letters and numbers, that is, alphabet and mathematics. He too possessed a wooden plaque to write upon; those were the days when the concept of paper and pencil had not yet commenced. People used to try to write on wooden plaques blackened with the black carbon procured from the back of the pans, and on them we wrote with the help of reed quills. Even granite slates and slate pencils weren't in vogue, for us villagers.

One day it so happened that, as usual, I was waiting for my classmate to accompany me to the school at his residence. I was waiting and he was making us late by not getting ready yet. Actually he had woken up late and her mother was busy preparing him for the school including making him eat something – sort of breakfast. I was getting thus late, too, in the process. Finally, when he got ready and we were to start for the school, I with the intention to loosen my muscles of hand strained due to holding the heavy plaque for long – by the standards of a kid – raised my hand above my head holding the plaque in my hand. Unintentionally, it gave the impression to my mate as if I was trying to hurt him with my plaque and the same impression was picked by the mother and other grandees of the house. I was bewildered by this implied sense of an innocuous action taken by the playmate and the elders. The child also raised his plaque in self-defence and a scene was created where two toddlers were pitched against each other ready to hurt themselves using the wooden plaques as weapons. The fact of the matter was that both of us were scared and were worried about hurt to ourselves and were aspiring for the intervention of someone elder. We were not being able to decide how this scene had been created out of an unintentional action on the part of a kid, simply raising his hand holding his writing plaque. The universe is made like that! The intentions of doers do seldom matter; instead, the implications and notions assigned by the other party matter. I was wondering why my friend interpreted my raising the plaque as my intention to hurt him.

Fortunately for us, the elder lady teacher saw us in that panicky situation and other household ladies too caught sight of this childish nightmare. They intervened just in the nick of the hour, lest we should have broken our skulls. When the elders intervened we felt relieved, and once again we were friends and went to school together. Without any malice in our hearts! The life of a child is very risky in that sense.

The lesson I learnt from that incident was that people - even our close friends - might interpret our actions otherwise, quite contrary to our intentions. I decided as well that when two persons are pitched against each other, it is quite possible that they might have fallen prey to the circumstances and might be craving intervention by someone to loosen the strings of rift and put them at rest. Not all the tiffs are intentional, most of the tiffs and squabbles are the by-products of indirect unintentional actions. It is therefore incumbent upon the bystanders and silent spectators to intervene in such scuffles that seem to be innocuous.

XXX

7. *Need Of* Chaar Aanaa *& A Child's Huge Bewilderment*

Enter Protagonist

Village *Paathshaalaa* was alright and I was enjoying my study in it, as also, the glory I had earned so easily, almost providentially thereat. I was, however, harbouring the notion by that time that the school was providing us the literacy gratuitously just like all other bounties of Nature – water, air, soil, trees, fire and space – that Nature afforded us free of cost, which we could use as much as we needed. By the same analogy, I entertained the notion that human enterprise and performance should as well be free of cost. I thought, I was being lettered without charging anything; how could a child after all know? Of course, the sisters in the *Paathshaalaa* used to do roll-call daily and the little kids responded to that enthusiastically which I craved very much: my name must be called, too. Nonetheless, I was never called on the roll. The reason was that I was not admitted to the *Paathshaalaa* formally; I was attending the school on the strength of clout my family entertained in the village and the poor ladies – sisters of the school – could not resist this illegality, for they were residing in the households pertaining to us for stay at this vulgar village. How circumstances could compel one to mould the laws and succumb to pressures of local strongmen as well as lumpens!

As I told earlier, the sisters kept on changing in the school quite frequently, as is the case even today: the resourceful teachers posted to rural areas – particularly ladies – use their connections for getting transferred to cozy places or to places nearby their homes. Even, some of them who hailed from the families having some higher officials in Govt or elsewhere, could afford to not attend the school at all regularly: they could simply go once or twice a week or on the day of collecting their wages only. This was not peculiar to those times; this is rampant even today. The major portion of amount being spent on primary education, especially in Govt schools, in India is going waste in this way; those teachers treat their employment merely as a means to mitigate their financial difficulties, not as a service to make the human race literate and cultured.

My situation was bizarre: I was not a regular student, my name was not called on the rolls; however, I paid the fees of the school as was assured by my father to the lady teachers of the *Paathshaalaa*. The fees was *'Chaar Aanaa'* (twenty five *paise*)! Sounds quite a trifling! And indeed it was! It was merely a token of imbibing in little souls the sense of belonging to the world of literacy, that is, the school.

Nonetheless, this paltry sum of twenty five *paise* was not an affordable sum in my household. Wondering? And thinking that I am playing sympathy card, what they call in politics – victim card? Unfortunately, that's not true – the wonderment and the allegation! Once my *Behenjee* asked me to pay the *chaar aanaa* and she repeated the

demand many a time, and I could not oblige for days together. Schools have some specific days for collection of fees and sensibly so, for they cannot waste all the days and all the sessions for such trifling as collection of fees. It is not that I did not ask my mother for giving me the money; I insisted on getting money daily before going to school and I told my mother that I felt humiliated in front of other classmates when the sister demanded fees and I had to cut a sorry figure. The teacher somehow felt that I had forgotten and did not demand of my parents, for the impression was that my parents as well as my family were quite well-to-do, rather, rich people. This was a hypocrisy and the reality was just the converse. My mother kept on parting with twenty five *paise* monthly out of her stock of money availed from her parents as a farewell gift when she departed from her father's home. And I entertained the notion that money was an ever available a commodity like water which was available on tap, nay, not on tap for taps were not in vogue those days, at least in villages; water was easily available in pitchers. Child as I was! The mother did not have even *chaar aanaa* that day since she had not been to her father's for quite a long time and her husband had usurped or, so to say, squeezed the last pie from her bones by at times wielding stick on her back, or at times boxes on her temples, or simply slapping her rapaciously.

There was no question of asking for fees from that rogue of a soul! He was not supposed to give anything; he was born for taking or grabbing everything for his individual person's sake; and for this conduct of his, he had no compunctions or qualms of conscience at all. At all! Like creatures of animal world!

Finally, one day I refused to go to school protesting that I felt humiliated, that my classmates thought that I was a poor boy, not able to afford even *chaar aanaas* despite claiming to be belonging to a great pedigree. My mother was hugely upset, but what could she do; she was helpless!

However, I wondered; we had so many blood relations all around us and they seemed to be quite affable and helpful towards us, yet could they not contribute even *chaar aanaas* towards the payment of fees of a little child. What sort of a relationship was that then, I so conspicuously wondered. It was all sham, I realised. One had to fend for oneself even amidst this seemingly own oasis of family and relations: our deserts were only our own!

Mother did not think even to seek help from my immediate elder aunt – *Tai*, I don't know why!

Ultimately, when I was so sentimentally upset, my mother struck upon a stratagem. In our front, there was the household of one of our grandpa's brothers – very large family, with very large habitats and courtyards. There lived an old lady who was very aged and quite fat. We called her '*Motee Ammaa*'. She was reportedly, as also, seemed to be very kind-hearted and good-demeanoured. My mother thought her to be the point of last resort. She being very seasoned seemed to be the only person who could protect our prestige and help us financially in this grave difficulty, of not having a *chavannee, chaar aanaas*! Not having a big sum may not be as humiliating a prospect as not having even a *chavannee* ; pettier the sum, sharper the dent to the prestige of a household!

My mother suggested that I should approach *Motee Ammaa* for lending me *chaar aanaas* explaining to her that I needed the same for paying my fees, that my teachers were demanding it for days together, and that I felt humiliated at the school in front of the children. This was for the first time that I was being made to suffer the ignominy of supplicating before someone for begging some money! That too, only a *Chavannee, Chaar Aanaas*! I protested to my mother contending that it was their duty to beg, not mine, and that it was very shameful of them that they could not afford even as petty a sum as *chaar aanaas!*

But to no avail! To no effect! Such eloquences become effective only on the sensible people; on duffers and madcaps, any sort of harangue of wisdom goes only waste. And it did! I felt disgusted. Had no option but to perform this feat – ignominy – of begging money from someone, however, related or aged. Summoning courage somehow and making my heart strong, and after rehearsing the monologue umpteen number of times before my mother, when my mother – the acting director – approved of my action, I ventured to the high elevated platform or high land of the household just in front of ours.

As soon as I stepped out of my corridor, I sighted the *Motee Ammaa* just in front of me, sitting in the sunshine and enjoying her morning respite and calm. I felt guilty of having to design against her calm and quietude. Not only this, she was surrounded by her grandchildren who were busy making mischiefs or doing sort of various errands all around. An additional complication was added to my venture thus: how to overcome this knot, how to crack this nut? In our scheme of things, we had envisaged that the grandma would be sitting all alone and I would be all alone, too, to somehow utter my lines of monologue which I had conned heartily.

Nevertheless, the adversity sharpens the faculties of brain!

This was quite a matter of shame for me – a child - to beg for as petty a sum as *chaar aanaas* before my playmates: how should I in future raise my head with self-esteem before them? Poverty is such a shame! Such a demeaner, such a demotivator! Nonetheless, for my father it was not, it mattered little: begging was his pet hobby! He had become sort of shameless in this behalf.

My mother suggested that I should whisper in the ears of *Motee Ammaa* my demand. I summoned my courage again, more so, because of the even bigger and graver shame that awaited me at school just after a few hours. I staggered towards their house; the children thought that I had come for playing or sitting in the sunshine to ward off the chill of winter. Before they could greet me and offer me participation in their games, I proceeded towards the grandma surreptitiously. She looked towards me inquisitively; I put my mouth touching and covering her ear and whispered, "*Ammaa*, give me *chaar aanaas*, my mother has asked, for I have to pay my school fees and my teachers humiliate me daily for this small sum at school!"

I can still today recollect this sentence so vividly; it had engraved such a dent on my heart! The grandmother was bemused first, even as, she could not hear or understand what I was whispering or what my intent was. More than hers, the children around her started making a fool of me and playing pranks upon me, "Are you trying to kill our *Ammaa*, *Eh*? What are you up to?" *blah blah*. All were party to that merry-making, opportunity for them and embarrassment for me. I felt benumbed.

I was not prepared for such an eventuality, nor had I envisaged that the situation could take such an embarrassing turn. I could not decide what to do and not being sure whether the grandma meant helping me or not, I thought it expedient to run away from the scene. The kind lady, however, called me back and instructed one of her senior daughters-in-law to heed me, understand me and give whatever little I had demanded from her. I explained my misery to the other lady, too - she was also my grandmother, however, *motee ammaa* was great grandmother to me. The other lady gave me *chaar aanaas*, holding which in my little fist, I rushed towards my home to the booing and hooting by the fellow playmates – 'you intended to murder our *Ammaa*' – and felt a sense of great achievement, *déjà vu* that I have never felt in my life thereafter again.

XXX

Table of Contents

8. A Prodigy Is Born:
Enter Protagonist

Now, at this later stage, I feel that those two little sisters at village school encouraged me by praising genuinely and whole-heartedly and holding me in specially high esteem. That helped boost my morale and, in turn, the potency of brain-power. Praise *per se* has a great gift of elevating everything, it broadens the mind and sharpens the brain! I shall always be thankful to those two little angelic sisters. They were the daughters of a shopkeeper of our village who was a progressive minded person and used to educate his daughters, that's why those two girls were quite brilliant whereas the ladies and girls in our households including our *Buaajee* and the related *Buaajees* were all almost illiterate and thumb-users. That was the bane of feudalistic mind-set, of *Talibaanee* mindset set up during *Muslim* rule of millennia.

Whereas I was enjoying my newfound phenomenon of what they call praise and glory and the resultant exhilaration in my heart and supposedly high esteem in the eyes of villagers, I discovered that gradually the euphoria of setting up schools in villages dissipated and the lady teachers all managed to get themselves transferred elsewhere, to their choice places, instead of remaining at our school, haunted by depraved lads and their equally vulgar elders. A time eventually came when there remained only one teacher who was comparatively an adult and of much advanced age. The same lady who lived in the household of one of our grandfathers. But she did not seem to be happy either.

I had become hero of my *Paathshaalaa*, but *Paathshaalaa* itself was about to be shut.

Before it could be shut, my father shifted me to the nearby town: to an *Aadarsh* Primary *Paathshaalaa*! In my child-like curiosity I could not decide why my father opted to shift me to the town which was almost two and a half kms away from our village and, to which, we had to walk on foot daily to and fro, whereas already there was a school in our own village which was quite in the vicinity of our house and where we could reach within a minute and could also come running home to have food or to drink water or to convey the happy augury in real time to my beloved mother that the teacher praised me for writing correctly.

When I was shifted to the town school, I felt bad and saddened, to be true. How do the adults behave I could not reconcile to, easily. As against the village *Paathshaalaa* and the affable behaviour of the sisters thereat, here, at the town school, the attitude of the teachers – all male – was indifferent and cold, just like the adults in our household. I thought how good it felt in our *Paathshaalaa*

where I got the praise of sisters! There, at the *Paathshaalaa*, I had established myself as a child prodigy – a born prodigy – whereas at this town school, there were a large number of students and there were many classes; back at our *Paathshaalaa* we didn't know that there was such a phenomenon, viz; something like 'classes' or 'grades' that segregated students as per their level or standard of learning. At our *Paathshaalaa,* all children squatted together on the floor, and there used to be only one class, or it seemed to be so to my child's senses. In our perception, in our perspective! Of course, there might have been different classes, i.e.; grades, but since the number of students was very few and the teachers were one or two only, they might be making everybody to sit together and might be assigning disparate tasks to students of different grades.

In our village *Paathshaalaa*, there was no question of giving corporeal punishment to students, but here, at town school, the teachers wielded the stick on the soft palms of the erring or naughty students, and also, they made them to assume the posture of a cock. Later on in life, I came to realise that the cock posture was a *Yoga* posture intended to sharpen the faculties of brain, however, administered as a punishment in schools.

In our village *Paathshaalaa*, I

had an innate sense of language and the teachers realised this and praised me, but at town school, I wondered, why the male teachers were so duffer as not to recognise my worth and the giftedness. The reason was, they were not connected with the students. They were not interested in identifying the specific skills of kids. They were simply teachers, the wage earners, Govt servants!

Nonetheless, whenever we rushed towards the town along with other students of the same age, we felt proud thinking that we studied in *Aadarsh* Primary *Paathshaalaa*, which was erroneously written as '*Aadrash* Primary *Paathshaalaa*' which mistake I did notice and used to bring the same to the notice of my classmates quite frequently; however, they were not amused, nor could they fathom what I meant. They could not make out that placement of 'r' from fourth place to third place changed the pronunciation of the word drastically. And that signified the beauty of the language, the *Deva-Naagaree* script! I used to pronounce the wrong word and the correct pronunciation and tried to expound the subtle difference between the right and wrong pronunciation to my fellow students, however, to be booed only.

It was not literally an *Aadarsh Paathshaalaa*, which means an ideal school, even though my father in his whims and fancies might

be thinking it to be so! Its name only was '*Aadarsh*' and nothing turned ideal unless in action it proved to be ideal whether it be a person or an institution.

XXX

9. Gopaal Panditjee *And My Intentional Bouts Of Slumber*

Enter Protagonist

My father was a teacher in the town, that is why I think he might have thought it expedient to shift me to the town school; he had little faith in the wisdom of the lady teachers teaching in our village *Paathshaalaa*. That was also a typical characteristic of feudal thinking: demeaning the ladies and rustic milieu in every respect.

Nevertheless, my father was not contented even with the style of teaching of *Aadarsh Paathshaalaa* inasmuch as he made me take tuitions from one *Panditjee – Gopaal panditjee* – who, hailing although he did from our hamlet, had shifted his residence to the town, possibly thinking oneself superior to the rustic villagers. He was a teacher, too, and was renowned for his tuitions, particularly for small kids, at initial stages. His cursive writing skills were famous – *Khushkhatee, Sulekh* as they called it. My father had a notion that if I did not take tuitions from *Gopaal panditjee* I would not be able to become expert in cursive and beautiful writing, or I might not be lettered properly, and that I should remain unlettered in that eventuality; *Gopaal panditjee* seemed to have that sort of mysterious if only abstract repute. It was sort of inevitability to become a disciple of *Gopaal panditjee* for becoming a wise and gifted person. I too had thus to have that baptism with *Gopaal panditjee's* fire!

As against the impression given me by my parents that *Gopaaljee* was an affable person, I found him quite cold towards me: at that age, I feel, I was inclined to treating or branding everybody having cold attitude towards me, if one did not explicitly show affection towards me. In the same vein, incidentally, I had declared that my maternal grandfather – *Naanaajee* – too was cold towards me. *Gopaaljee* was at least not affable, he was sort of indifferent and strict – by the standards and aspirations of a small child. Incidentally, his spot of giving tuitions was a balcony or a porch or a veranda of a shopkeeper in the town and in the background, or so to say, all around there, there was a constant buzz of shopping and trading activity going on all the time. In that noisy atmosphere, *Gopaal panditjee* taught us, gave us tuitions! And people contended that he was very wise and bright; even a small child could discern this blunder in *Gopaal panditjee's* perspective as regards teaching or giving tuitions to kids!

As for me, *Gopaaljee* wrote with soft chalk the alphabets – *kitkinnaa* -- on my wooden plaque and I used to trace them with my liquid solution of calcium – white chalk. I was quite able to do that inasmuch as I had already learnt that much, courtesy of my illiterate mother's initiation and the feats shown by me at my village *Paathshaalaa*. Well, when I got shifted to the town school, many of our householders and some villagers, too, raised objections and asked questions to my father why I had hurt the sentiments of the nestling village school, contending that if the children of our own households did not study in the village school whose children would study there and ultimately the school – which was possibly opened after strenuous efforts of some progressive-minded villagers – would cease to function, in the absence of disciples. Nevertheless, it made no impact on my father's thinking. He did not want his scion to be taught in a rustic environ! Again a hollow feudal mind-set!

Because *Gopaaljee* had several other disciples, as well, like me, I felt he paid little attention to me and was a bit harsh towards me; I soon got wearied of this environment: it was not an atmosphere suitable for studies, I felt. I used to wait for the lunch break and at times even used to start having my lunch without waiting for the lunch-break permitted by *Panditjee*, to the amusement and derision of one and all of my mates who used to take tuitions there. They interpreted my actions as those of a duffer and idiot; and it hurt me, because at my *Paathshaalaa*, I was already a proven prodigy. And here, at *Gopaal panditjee's* tuition centre, pecuniary *Gurukul*, I was being treated and declared as a duffer – a *Buddhoo*, a *Baawaraa*. Getting wearied, I started sleeping during the classes, too, stretching my legs nonchalantly and sleeping, as though I were sleeping at my home; this I did on purpose; I simply pretended to be sleeping. When *Panditjee* saw me asleep, he would ask the other children to wake me up and they tried their best to wake me up, even by sitting on my tummy and back, but I would not budge or wake up. One could wake up a sleeping person but one could not wake up a person who was pretending to be asleep. This proverb was proving to be enacted in full force in this case; and I could taste the sweetness of this proverb. While doing all this, I however was afraid that *Panditjee* would get angry and report my misdemeanour to my father; also, that my father would get angry with me; and out of this fear also I did not gather courage to come to senses and wake up. I wanted to hide my head like an ostrich which the latter proverbially does in the

sand, that is, with an intention of avoiding reality that was glaring in my face.

The message was conveyed to my father as was expected; and I do not recollect any other episode which proves that I continued to study there any further. I was back to the precincts of *Aadarsh Paathshaalaa* where there was no compulsion of studying or tracing of alphabets – *kitkinnaa*. The Govt teachers were least concerned about whether the children got lettered or remained unlettered, or whether they wrote beautifully or shoddily; their salary was sure to be paid.

However high might be the repute of *Gopal panditjee* in the area, my grandfather deflated the same in a mere pin-pricking sort of an anecdote. He disclosed to me later in life that *Gopaaljee* was a teacher in a primary school some time back. There under duress or due to greed of lucre he used to issue fake mark-sheets or *Sanad* (Certificate) to the disciples so as to help them seek employment in Govt, or admissions in higher educational classes. How shameful! This gory incident ultimately came to light and a criminal case got instituted against the erring and corrupt teacher by the police of *Goree* – British -- government. *Baabaa* also clarified that had it been like the present days, the police would have converted this unpardonable crime into a money churning contrivance for themselves: they would have extracted the desired amount of money from the teacher, the swindler, and would have let him go free, scot-free. That's so true! After all *Lakshmee* is more adorable than *Saraswatee* ; and greed is more preferable to justice and righteousness, to an unenlightened person!

"How did the hateful episode end ultimately?" I asked my grandfather curiously.

"*Gopaal* cried aloud like women before the *Munsif* (judge) and the latter under compunction of his heart punished *Gopaal* monetarily, however, dismissing him from the job, yet not sentencing him to prison."

"That's why he was giving tuitions to students!" I exclaimed. And I was assigned to a person for lettering me in *khushkhatee (*cursive writing) whose character itself was not above board and not beautiful. Not *khushkhat* (worth writing, praise-worthy)!

XXX

Enter Protagonist

As I have narrated already, whenever my indolent natured father faced the shortage of food at his household, rather, it should be said like this: whenever he was unable to afford food and cereals for his ever enlarging family, he resorted to the easiest way out of this calamity by simply despatching his contingent to his in-law's house, that is, our *Nanihaal*. Studying even as I used to be at the town school – village *Paathshaalaa* having already gone beyond my bounds which I missed a lot – I along with my mother found myself in the village of my *Naanee* quite often. By that time, in my mind, there was no conception of the continuity of the session or of the certain minimum percentage of the attendances required for continuing one's studies in an educational institution, that is, school. I, in my childish conviction, assumed that all the schools were open to all the children and any child whosoever could go attend any school anywhere throughout India at his sweet will. Therefore, it never occurred to me when I reached my *Nanihaal* that my studies had been interrupted due to my father's having shunted us towards his in-laws mid-session. Here too, the children of our maternal uncles – my cousins of almost the same age as I – used to go to the school that was available in the nearby small village called *Naglaa Kath*.

In fact there was no building of that school as such and, instead, the school was run at the mercy of a benevolent villager whose open air platform was quite large and there were shaded trees, as well, to protect the children from the scorching sunshine. Thus, we studied under the trees *a la Shaanti Niketan,* even as, we did not know the name and concept of *Shaanti Niketan* by that time. Nonetheless, the compulsions and constraints of schools had availed for us the experience of *Gurudeva's* concept of *Shaanti Niketan* albeit unbeknown to us yet.

We were enjoying our studies, and also, felt a sense of freedom, a sense of freedom from cares of any sort. Our teacher here was a male named *Qutubuddeen.* He was a nice and sober teacher -- as I can now vouchsafe when I have come of age as well as senses -- and also, of quite the young age: we kids liked him. However, one day, I was making noise and mischief and was not behaving; I might have been in some mirthful mood. The teacher rebuked me and in the process slapped me softly in the face, too. Softly or hardly, it was immaterial, but the humiliation of having been punished by the teacher was material and an issue of grave concern for me -- a pampered child of wealthy background insofar as my maternal relations were concerned! How could a teacher, that too, a *Muslim,* punish the child who was a guest for the village, a guest of honour, sort of – the son of a gifted lady! I started crying and shouting awkwardly as had been my habit since time

unknown. Along with me started shouting the other kids of my clan, that is, my maternal cousins and all other kids of our *Nanihaal.* Shouting at the teacher, our Master! Can anyone imagine? Even at that young age we had the temerity to resent the punishment meted out to a child by an alien sort of a teacher who came from some other village and taught us at that hamlet. All of us rose up in protest and left the school – the make-shift school – shouting aloud and malignantly, '*Qutubuddeen Badaa Kameen! Totaa Maare Saadhe Teen!*' and we chanted this derogatory slang or song, whatever one would like to call it, for quite a while. To this obscenity on our part some other sensible and seasoned villagers of the hamlet took offence; they sided with the teacher and rightly so, as I now think in hindsight, and chided us. We felt bad at their approach – the approach of villagers: they should have supported us, we thought; after all they were from our village! There ought to have been the fellow feeling at display, we thought. The teacher got embarrassed. We left the school. The teacher also ordered us out and to leave the school forthwith.

When we reached our *Nanihaal* weeping and crying and shouting, our elders took notice. As usual, the most ferocious entity – our elder *Maamaajee* -- took command and the lead. He headed towards the school, the nearby village, to accost the erring teacher. We followed him, too. *Maamaajee* on reaching the make-shift school, took up the issue with the teacher and sort of reprimanded him saying that his nephew -- the son of his youngest sister -- whether he studied or not, it was none of his business – teacher's business – and that the teacher had no right to punish me, his nephew. Incidentally, ours was the largest contingent in the school and the remaining students were very few after we left. We therefore thought, the teacher would come to his knees! We still cursed *Qutubuddeen* that the school would be closed, God willing, within no time! But it didn't, thankfully so, for after a few years thereafter I had to seek refuge for my education to this school only. That episode, however, sometime later when the occasion arises. Towards this aim, i.e. to make the school shut shop immediately, we induced the remaining children to leave the school but they did not budge; rather, they found fault with us only, to our disappointment and first taste of social norms and inter-relationships. We could not decide why they – the villagers and their wards -- did not follow suit and support us.

Thus, our short tryst with *Qutubuddeen's Paathshaalaa* came to an abrupt end! While leaving the school with our *Maamaajee* we dared *Qutubuddeen* that we would take admission in *Jaabil* school. The fault of the poor yet righteous teacher was that he had beaten a bright boy for the latter was making childish mischiefs!

XXX

Table of Contents

11. Shifted To Jaabil. The Land Of Jaabaali

Enter Protagonist

From the next day, we were sent to the *Jaabil* school. Here, too, the school had no building of its own as such. It was also run in the open, or under a shaded veranda at the place of some villager – a rich one. However, at *Jaabil,* we found that the school used to get shifted from place to place quite frequently: at least four or five spots we can still recollect where the school got shifted during our short stint at that school. At times it so happened that when we reached the school where it was running the previous day, we found that the school had been shifted elsewhere to someone else's household. It was such a shifting sands sort of experience in the educational set-up in those days that we children were facing and were baffled at the failure of the system. Nevertheless, we were unperturbed by all these rapid changes, even as, we did not know the implications and reasons of those quick changes in location of the school at *Jaabil*. Might be due to the weariness and insolence of the owners of the places. After all in a children's school lot of noise and mischief in the name of merry-making is always there! In countryside, the people are excessively possessive about their land-holdings and places, that is, shelters.

First, the teacher at *Jaabil* school got happy in that he had got some more students, but later on, when he came to know, and we narrated to him with vitriolic fervour why we had left the *Naglaa Kath* school and how we had cursed *Qutubuddeen* there, the teacher did not take this malignancy of our childish hearts towards his clan of teachers favourably; his attitude towards us underwent change unfavourably. He kept us as students though and did not rusticate us. At *Jaabil* school, our enthusiasm was not that high as this was at *Naglaa Kath*. This school was a bit farther and we had to eat our food – lunch -- midway before reaching there.

Ultimately, after testing the shades and soils of almost half a dozen households, the school was shifted to the well-head of the ramshackle school building which itself was not habitable and safe. The days were those of winter season; therefore, sitting in sunshine gave a salubrious and soothing feeling to us children, yet sitting at the well-head always posed a risk of falling down in the well. Moreover, in my subconscious mind I still retained the memory of my fall from the well-head in my village, whose scar was still there present on my skull. We, therefore, took extreme care not to venture near the well or to peep inside it as did other kids do. We wondered how a teacher could take the risk of making the children sit beside such a grave risk as sitting near the well in which someone might fall inadvertently!

Which class it was I cannot recollect. However, we can recollect that after sometime the school of *Qutubuddeen* was shut temporarily and we were left with no other school but that of *Jaabil* only. Almost a dozen or so children commuted to the *Jaabil* school daily. There was no risk either of any beast or any man on the way who could deprive us of our lives or possessions. One thing, of course, we remember yet: *Jaabil* was a larger village and we had a shop there – a provision store – all sorts of stuff worthy of children's interest were found there. We took an amount of cereals from our *Naanee*'s house clandestinely in our bags and used that quantity in barter for purchasing some trifling from the shop. The old man who was quite benevolent as well used to give us some home-made digestive globules or tablets which used to be very tasty. People those days were very considerate and kind and they could not think of selfishness, or of harming others, that's my impression. They knew what was good for the children's health and for society at large.

Sometimes when we the children haggled and quarrelled with him – and we did it quite often as it gave us poetic pleasure -- the old man rebuked us in mock irritation. *Jaabil* village had become like our own habitat in a sense. Those were the days of innocence and without any risks involved as have evolved with the degenerative political practices and are prevalent these days permeating the whole social milieu of our land.

In the rainy season when there used to be waterlogging all around in the fields, we had to traverse and wade through the puddles and there was every danger of snakes and reptiles accosting us on the pavement. Our elders used to forewarn us that there might be any snake or something dangerous on the pavement we treaded, and that we had to mind our steps while stepping ahead and not to deviate from the paved beaten path, since the reptiles were supposed to dread the pavements and the sound of foot-steps. To ward off the risk of serpents and water creatures, we therefore used this foot-patting strategy continuously throughout the journey to *Jaabil* school. We were sure in this way that the serpent would not come rushing to attack us by this strategem: this was like a *Paritraan Mantra (Paritta)* for us in the parlance of lord *Buddha!*

Fortunately, we never met with any such serpentine dread or danger on our path. Something above us might be protecting us innocent and simple-hearted children! Otherwise too, the creatures of Nature except *homo sapiens* do not attack anybody without any cause. Entire Nature is governed like that only: there is no effect without a cause in the Creation. Entire Creation is the game of cause and effect only! However, this truism doesn't apply to the demeanour of human beings!

XXX

12. Bhaaloo Waalee Kitaab - And (Bearish Pranks)

Enter Protagonist

Even as I don't know which class or standard I was in when I used to go to *Jaabil* school – the make-shift school – so to say, yet I have one memory intact in my brain in that respect.

Again, as usual, I was in my *Naanee's* village and attending the primary school at the nearby village called *Jaabil*: without any formal admission and without any sanctity of my studies. Yet I was a bright boy – an acknowledged one -- as I had linguistic grasp and sharpness of comprehension as regards the language. I am talking of language, not the numbers and the complications associated therewith, which I shall dwell upon at appropriate time. Seeing my unusual brightness and given the status of wealth of my maternal grandfather, the teachers could not forbid me from attending the school without any formal registration; they had been briefed duly that I was there only for time being, only by the time my father called me and my mother back to his village.

There are some incidents which, notwithstanding their seemingly appearing to be trifling, leave an indelible imprint on the mind and heart! Now, take for instance the *'Praveshikaa'*, the Elementary Primer, the class which we called as *'Bhaaloo Waalee'* class, that is, the initiating class for schooling. Therein there was a rhyme, concerning a bear, reading as follows:

> A bear does come
> With a stick in hand
> Making sounds like,
> *Chham, chham, chham,*
> *Chham, chham, chham*

All the same again, the venue of this tale is our *Nanihaal* only: *Naanaa*'s house. Presently, when we are discoursing on the *'Praveshikaa'*, how old I would have been at that time, can be guessed quite easily: hardy five years old. Yet, even after so many decades having elapsed in the interregnum, every detail of the episode is so clear as if I have arisen from sleep after seeing a dream.

About how the children can make unintentional mischief and noise!

I was in the *'Bhaaloo Waalee Kitaab'* class, or grade as they call it now; that's why I say that I can't vouchsafe for the number aspect of learning. It was *'Bhaaloo Waalee Kitaab'* class for me; I had possibly cleared the elementary six pager book of alphabet, which was available at the grocer's shop at our village, being sold along with the digestive powder – *haazmaa choorna* - - and the jaggery. Now, since I had read and finished that small booklet for quite a long while, and also, practised tracing the *kitkinnaa* on my wooden plaque quite satisfactorily, I was supposed to learn something further and that next thing was the *Bhaaloo Waalee Kitaab*. Nevertheless, I didn't possess that book or booklet yet; how to avail that booklet was a big issue for me, the child. While buying the primer from the grocer's shop at our village, I had never imagined in the wildest dreams of mine that there could be any other book in the world than that one. Book meant book for me: why two; one book ought to suffice to teach everything to anyone! To make anyone literate! Or, to make anyone educated, cultured, I mean, if that's the destined aim of all this rigmarole called learning the letters and numbers! I didn't know by that time that it was an immeasurable wilderness! Going unto infinity! This world of books and learning! Like the infinite sky!

Nonetheless, the reality was otherwise. The initiation into letters could be only gradual and the learning could never be assumed to have been completed while living on this planet; this realisation, of course, came quite late in my life when I turned what they call 'senile' and could think in fact 'sanely'.

How to get the '*Bhaaloo Waalee Kitaab*' was a great conundrum for me; the teacher had commanded me to come up with the next book apart from the basic primer. The ultimate refuge for a child: the mother's lap! On returning from the *Paathshaalaa*, I bumped into the belly of my mother and asked, "*Beebee*, where shall I get *Bhaaloo Waalee Kitaab*? *Maassaab* has commanded me to come up with that book next time."

Against my apprehension that the mother would get perturbed or would get worried to hear this, the mother showed no concern. However, that unconcern for my demand could be interpreted in two ways: either the mother was least bothered about my well-being and educational anxieties, or the mother thought this issue quite a trivial one, not worth warping the eyebrows about or straining the lines of her forehead about.

When I showed my desperation, the mother opened up and said, "Alright, you will get one; next time when *Naanaajee* goes to the town he will bring the book." I felt surprised how the shopkeeper would know that I needed a *Bhaaloo Waalee Kitaab*; how he could have prepared one in advance for our *Naanaajee* to purchase the same. Anyway, this mystery continued until *Naanaajee* made it to the town as usual for purchase of monthly or fortnightly provisions, and in the evening when he returned, I was the first person to await with bated breath the arrival of my precious possession: the *Bhaaloo Waalee Kitaab*.

It's at that point that *Naanaajee* was sighted coming back from *Khurjaa* – the nearby city or town – clad in a loose and lengthy *Kurtaa* of *Khaadee* cloth, along with white *Dhotee* wrapped around the waist, and with a scarf wrapped around the skull. He used to visit the nearby town – *Khurjaa* – once in a while for fetching the monthly provisions for the household.

All of us kids did gather around *Naanaajee* out of curiosity.

In the sprawling courtyard of the mansion-like house *Naanaajee* did take out the provisions from his bag one by one.

Naanaajee did not give the book immediately or straightaway, nor did he take out the book as a first item from his shopping sack; rather, he took out all other items first, and then took out the book only at the fag-end, as the last item, last surprise.

I can still recall to my memory chip so well, on the occasion of the arrival of *'Bhaaloo Waalee Kitaab'*, I and my mother coupled with the company of other members of the big household had cheered the moment. Chanting with a chuckle *'Laathee lekar bhaaloo aayaa!'* *Naanaajee* had handed me the book with much graceful gesture, 'Do take your *Bhaaloo Waalee Kitaab!* A primer for a bear!'

My mother handed me the book with great affection and aspirations as though with that *Bhaaloo Waalee Kitaab* I was going to metamorphose from a bear into a human species.

Nevertheless, on this development, I should have been elated; but there were sitting other children of my maternal uncle who were elder to me. I thought of celebrating and relishing the arrival of my new book by creating some histrionics; and the best and most gratuitous histrionic for a child is to cry or squeak without any cause, so as to draw attention of the elders, so as to look special and extraordinary. To express my gaiety, I started weeping or squeaking in mock style without any substance and sincerity therein. To the amazement of all present! I too felt awkward; why I should have behaved like that whereas nothing untoward had happened to me! But child is a child:

he wanted to draw attention, and he drew it through this crazy medium. The elders assuaged me genuinely by telling that I had got my cherished book, for which, I had been craving for quite some time, then why should I have been making a fuss. My elder lady cousin recited *Bhaaloo Waalee Kavitaa* from the book; and I recited after her, emulating her; and thus came to an end my misdirected and ill-conceived histrionics.

Unreasonable actions on the part of children can be expected; they can play such tricks whenever they feel neglected, or even when they want to draw attention of the elders.

Naanaajee relished playing with children and mainly fooling them. We were fond of going to a nearby brook – an irrigation channel -- for taking a dip therein. There used to be no concern for the weather conditions whether it be summer, sunny, sweltering or raining. *Naanaajee* once tried to dissuade us by warning, 'Today, I saw a very big sized creature wading through the brook heading towards *Khurjaa*, that is, in the opposite direction of the water's current and flow, so large was its mouth that entire body of water was getting sucked inside its wide mouth, and that it was filling the entire breadth of the brook by its demoniac body, and that its speed was so ferocious, just can't tell.' It was just fitting in the concept of a dragon.

Innocent kids! How could they discern what the truth was and what the lie was? All did assemble around the cot of the old grandee, with their mouths agape, 'Why, *Baabaa*, was it really going through the brook?'

'What do you think, I am telling a lie?', *Naanaajee* chastised them with mirthful chuckle.

Simultaneously beckoning to his elder brother – the elder maternal grandfather – he exclaimed emphatically, 'Brother! It was a very big beast!'

'Oh!' Elder *Naanaajee* too distorted his face in mock astonishment; simply for the sake of us kids.

XXX

13. Clay, Craft And Calamity
Enter Protagonist

Bhaaloo Waalee Kitaab, or *Jaabil,* or my *Naanee*'s village, all were but temporary phases; ultimately I had to return to my roost; to my roots, that is, the roots of my father, where he had in fact nothing virtually to call as his own. Yet, because the mother was married there she had to return there, time and time again.

And the school there was the *Aadarsh Paathshaalaa* at the nearby town as is already known.

I was taken as a duffer throughout in classes first, second and third, as I can recall quite vividly even today. I was only one of the melee, one in the crowd of the mediocre and buffoons. Teachers there seemed to be strict, or this was the impression I gathered from my child's perspective.

I don't know why I reminisce this episode till date. I can't even dub it as a nominal incident, for having happened in the very beginning of the life, this incident still survives in my mind; that also goes to suggest that there must be some exceptional significance or import of this incident, which I frankly don't know.

I might be studying in class one or two at the material time: at the most in class three. I frequented the dust-way from *Maar-Haraa*, my village, to *Jhaa-Jhar,* the town school, every day.

Incidentally, clay craft was in vogue in those days and was one of the subjects taught in schools. We were supposed to make various types of toys during exams with the sticky black clay which was abundantly available in the countryside in our area, particularly, in the village ponds called *Pokhar*.

Those were the exam days. One thing about the exams that fascinated me was that I loved the coloured question papers that the teachers distributed to the examinees. However, we being in the lower classes were never given any papers, neither coloured nor uncoloured. Nor could possibly we read those crispy and palm-sized papers for we were not completely lettered yet. Our exams used to be verbal only – for smaller kids, of lower grades. And that was a grave disappointment, particularly, for me! Why such ill-luck, only for me? When everybody else did get to get the coloured question papers!

On one such occasion, our strictest teacher, who hailed incidentally from our village only, and was notorious for his strictness and high pitched baritone voice, commanded us to come up with the clay toys next day for the examination of craft – the clay craft. That was a huge task – a great assignment -- for a small kid of standard one. My only recourse was my mother, and hers, in turn, were her sisters-in-law who were aplenty there in our inter-related households and joint family. On begetting issues there was no bar put yet by the world.

As for clay-craft, the teacher had asked the toddlers to make two or three idols of muddy soil: clay toys. I conveyed the grave as well as urgent message to my mother with added gravity that if I did not take the clay toys to school the next day, the so and so teacher would hang me, berate me, or beat me severely. My mother knew the falsity of this pretension but I as a child was sincere in my concern, even as, the impression about the teacher in our minds was

like that only.

I had therefore busied myself wholeheartedly in making the idols. After haggling with my lovely mother I had somehow made her to arrange some quantity of suitable sticky clay – *chiknee mittee* -- from somewhere in the village.

The mother took help of her sisters-in-law and got prepared the clay toys – two or three -- I can't recollect; and the same were put under the sun to dry up to some extent given the unfavourable condition of sunshine, it being the monsoon season. However, those were the days of monsoon and the sunrays were scarce. The toys did not dry up and were still soft and vulnerable.

It was only after the idols had been crafted, even though only wet yet, that I could derive solace of having solved the question of exam which loomed in my face alike the question of life and death. And it was only because of this accomplishment that I could sleep free of worries in the night.

I was enthused to take my clay craft work to school with utmost sincerity. However, the next day morning, when I woke up, I saw it was raining again, to my utter dismay and anxiety. It was raining cats and dogs – it was a downpour, rather. No question of going to school.

"What about my toys?" I enquired of my mother in a morose

tone as if my earnings of whole life had been lost, wiped off in a deluge. Well, if the toys prepared with so much exertion and after resolving so many issues did get destroyed in the rain, it was a valid reason for getting frustrated and depressed indeed. How much attached one feels towards one's creations, however childish, in the early age! Why only early age; at every juncture of age in life! How much affliction! The children are in fact the sources infinite of the creativity and originality. Crush this creativity and the same child would be transformed into a devil or a daemon.

"I have salvaged them by taking inside before it started raining." Mother replied.

"Nonetheless, those would be wet yet? My teacher may not award me any marks for the wet toys!" I sighed.

"He will! In this wet weather and rains, it's not only you, but all the kids will bring only the wet toys." My lovely mother assured me.

However, it was still raining when I was talking to my mother. How pathetic it would be that the toys prepared with so much love and labour would not eventually secure marks or due prestige in the school! How miserable!

My grandpa declared it a rainy day, incidentally, when he happened to visit the female residences in the morning for some daily chore; he was fond of declaring it a rainy day whenever two drops of water came down from the sky, to our amusement and relief. On a rainy day, we weren't supposed to go to school. But today was not a usual day, it was special in all respects, and the stakes were quite high; the risks were quite high: the command -- inviolable command -- of the tyrant teacher! How could we disobey his orders!

I insisted on going to school come what may. My mother tried to dissuade me but I didn't budge, 'My *maassaab* will flog me!' Finally, mother agreed and prepared me to go to school covering me under a polythene sheet, and the clay toys were wrapped, too, under the polythene.

It was a day of rains! A day of the monsoon season! How terrible the rain that day was! The water was pouring down in streams, or figuratively, from water drums, will be a more apt description of the scenario. Coupled with roaring and resonating uproar of the lightning and thunderstorm! Nonetheless, my exams were on! It couldn't be helped! It was the exam of clay-craft and handicraft scheduled for the day! Till even yesterday, the sky was absolutely clear and cloudless, without even a hint or smell of the impending rains the very next morning.

By the grace of God, the

intensity of the rains did subside a whit low, and my mother wrapping the wet toys carefully in a polythene did handover to me. I can recall to mind still: holding in one hand a clay glass and in the other a clay inkpot, I was pacing fast on the muddy path. The mother had stood there at the gate of the homestead for quite a while watching me from afar. Then when I turned round the corner, she could no longer watch me. A mother was watching her piece of heart with the eyes and gaze of extreme affection and attachment! And hearty prayers, I am sure! It was so that I was going to school insistently despite my mother trying to dissuade me from doing so! But how couldn't I? It was the matter of exam after all!

I can still recollect the day with such a vividness: I as a tiny toy was walking alone in the small alley of the village; there was no other soul around there in the village alley, and I was holding my treasure trove – the clay toys – in my hands, wholly wrapped in polythene; and my mother was standing worried at the gate of our thatched house, hugely worried and with throbbing heart, seeing her toddler straddling the village alleys all alone in that downpour. She had not been able to resist my penchant for attending the school; the scare of teacher prevailed upon the mother's caresses.

As soon as I turned round the corner, I looked back once more at my mother: she was still there. I could feel her heart beats and concern for me, having sent her piece of heart in this thunderstorm. One or two village people who met me on the way asked me why I had ventured out in such an inclement weather and my crisp response would be, 'I am going to take exam.' Exam for a toddler! It was indeed an exam for me!

The moment I was out of sight from my mother, it started raining cats and dogs again. Terrific downpour, so to say! I felt nonetheless enthused to think that despite the downpour my mother would no more be able to check me from going to school. I was covered under a rain-sheet, not a raincoat. All other students had possibly already gone. I was all alone on the way marching towards the town in that terrific rain and thunderstorm. Incidentally, at one spot on the way, I felt my legs quivering without a cause as though. For a moment I was befuddled, even as, I could not make any head and tail of this untoward happening on the way.

Later on, I was apprised by others that it was an earthquake, a severe one. The land had cleaved at some places, the homesteads had cracked in some cases. The people who conveyed this message to me also added emphatically that earthquake was a very bad ominous occurrence of Nature. We found that the wall of our school rooms had cracked, too. I being an ignoramus couldn't fathom anything; I had in fact surmised when it happened with me on the way that the ground from beneath my feet was giving way without any particular cause. I reached the school, only to be enlightened that very few kids had attended the school that day; also, those who had attended were, too, in the same wretched condition I was in – dripping, holding wet toys in their hands.

Once the sight of mother was hidden I was on my own. I found to my amazement that there was nobody on the muddy path from the village to the town; why should one be outdoors in such a weather!

Of course, when I reached outside the bounds of the village near an orchard, I found a swampy puddle and as a child out of curiosity I waded in it and suddenly felt that everything was shaking. I thought it was shaky ground that's why I was shaking, but later on I was given to understand that it was an earthquake and a high intensity one. Coupled with heavy downpour! However, in this shaky situation my clay toys got exposed to the rains directly, and also, were damaged to some extent and I felt sad, yet something was better than nothing, I thought. I had after all been able to salvage some of them! The *Maassaab* would give grace for precipitative circumstances! All along the way to my *Paathshaalaa* I

was harbouring the notion that my craft would be the best since my mother and my aunts had left no stone unturned to make them the best. I kept on imagining that as soon as I reached the school, my *Maassaab* would praise me like anything. Childish aspirations and wishful thinking!

Rainfall, thunderstorm, earthquake, what was not there on that day, that morning, on the way to the institution of learning that could not make a mother's heart tremble with terror for her only son: by that time I was her only son, the second one having already died, and other two having not yet arrived on the scene, possibly suffering their pangs in their old ages elsewhere yet.

My mother, later on, when I came back from the school, told me that she had been praying to God unceasingly when I was on way to school during that downpour and that she got extremely worried when the earth shook and that she lamented why she had permitted me to leave for school. Mother's cares!

This gesture of extreme affection shown by a mother I have never been able to let go to oblivion.

When I reached my *Paathshaalaa*, assuming that there would be nobody except me in the school, and that *Maassaab* would praise me for my valour of having attended the school even against all odds – those of downpour, of thunderstorm, of earthquake, all that -- I found to my consternation and pique that I was late, and that already almost all the students were present in their classes, and our tyrant *Maassaab* was sitting in his chair along with the only other teacher, of course, this time in a jolly and affable mood. When I approached him and unwrapped my clay craft in high aspirations of getting praise from him, both of them beckoned me to dump the toys in a corner where already the corpses of the equally pretty clay crafts of other children were piled up, all broken, all muddled as a lump of clay. That seemed to me as though the same was the fate of our lives; we would be dumped like clay craft some day at the command of someone obscure! However, expectant we may feel that we had done wonders and that people would praise us!

"*Maassaab!* Toys!", with enthusiasm as well as grace and with a feeling of pride as though I had won a battle, I exhibited my wares to the teacher and offered, expecting profuse praise in return, maximum marks in test – the test of nerves -- and thinking that the love and labour of my lovely mother and myself would be accomplished; however, this was not to be!

"Dump that side, in that nook!"

Immediately it struck me that all this was not as important as I was considering it to be; and that had I not attended the school that day, no sky would have fallen, too. The desperation we exhibit towards attainment of the desired results is but a madness only; nothing matters in absolute terms in this world. The same artefacts which I was valuing so much and so highly had in fact no worth in the eyes of my teachers – the duo who were sitting together there when I offered my pieces of heart to them.

I felt heart-broken at this treatment of my mother's labours and love, of my aunt's labours and love, and of all my risk taking feats during so many natural oddities prevalent on the day. The teachers were right and justified in their approach; nonetheless, in having trivialised the issue, and thus having set the children at ease; so that they needed not worry about the clay crafts in such abnormal circumstances; nevertheless, our aspirations and expectations from them were quite at divergence.

On returning home, when my mother asked me expectantly what the response of my teacher was on seeing my set of clay constructs, I responded morosely, 'he simply asked me to dump them in the lump of other toys!'

'Oh very sad! Love's labour lost! Then why did they instruct you kids to do all that labour in the first place?'

But now at this advanced stage, in my hindsight, I feel that all our anxieties, all our efforts, concerns, creations, crafts, possessions *et al* which we value so much and cherish so much, consider them so valuable, are in fact nothing, of no value, in the eyes of those who are not associated with them, least of all to the Creator of this Cosmos who has already created an inimitable and unprecedented craft of His own! The craft that keeps on renewing itself ceaselessly!

Figuratively, this is not the only episode of heart-break at that school; I had also got my skull hurt in that school once. Once when I was watching the elders of school practising gymnasium which involved wooden implements incidentally, when an elder boy was moving his hands violently around, I came in the range of his activity and the wooden ball that was stuck to the stick hit my skull and hurt me very excruciatingly. It was unbearable; still I bore it without weeping, but my skull thereafter became numb on that side and it continued for long. However, for fear of rebuke I did not bring this to the notice of my parents, least of all, the father, who was cruel, and instead of assuaging me, would have aggravated my misery by rebuking me, by adding fuel to fire; he was such sort of a callous and cruel person. I think neither the memory of that inexorable hurt in my skull has evaporated, nor the hurt; my skull on that side is as though permanently numbed.

XXX

Table of Contents

11. Ice Cream, Elders And My Innocence

Enter Protagonist

Of those hazy days, I have a few recollections like the spark of lightning. One such instance is that one day after the school was over and we were set free by the teacher for going to our villages -- our homes -- we the little children dispersed into the town market instead of heading towards our homes. I too followed suit, there being no other option; I was so small, I had to follow in the footsteps of the elder children only. I had no free-will or wisdom of my own in that respect.

Not far from the *Paathshaalaa,* the boys assembled at a nook where an ice-cream pedlar was already present with his enticements of not only ice-candies, but also, some attractive toys: of petty value, of course. Nonetheless, for children, that was a great attraction, particularly, on a hot summer noon.

I was blindly following the kids, having no craving or intentions of my own. The children started buying ice-candies and licking and sucking them, and I was simply watching them intently, without any desire to have ice-cream; I don't know why. Maybe, I was not having any *paise* with me; and also, I observed that the children were first offering *paise* to the pedlar and then only they were getting ice-cream, and that monetary realisation might have dissuaded me from even thinking of getting the ice-cream. Albeit that much sense I didn't have by that time! I might have realised by seeing all that, instead, that nothing was made available for free: even to innocent children.

Meanwhile, an old lady and her granddaughter, who were related to our family by some distant connection, happened to pass by at that moment. They sighted me standing there and watching the kids intently sucking the ice-sticks. Though I had no such feeling of deprivation or wretchedness in my heart on not getting to have the ice-cream, however, both the ladies felt pity towards me unbidden, and with great intensity which was expressed on their faces so conspicuously. They asked me condescendingly, rather, piteously, "You would like to have ice-cream, dear?" I, of course, getting embarrassed, replied in negation, yet the old lady was so kind-hearted that she forcibly bought a candy of ice-cream for me and handed it to me.

Why should I not have been pleased to have got this gratuitous gift of ice candy on a hot day? Nonetheless, I was feeling ill at ease on sucking it, also, thinking whether it was something of an aberration not to have even a single *paisaa* in my pocket as other kids were having and spending as per their sweet will and desire and satiating their ambitions and expanding their mental dimensions. But my parents had never thought on those lines possibly! They either could not afford such luxuries of spending money on childish ice-candies. Of course, how could they? I had quite often observed them squabbling for those *paise* only at my house. Mine was a queer household; and now I think in hindsight that my parents were, rather my father was, a queer creature in all such respects.

All was going well and I could not think that this seemingly trifling event in my school life could be such an important one and could have such grave implications for my family's and father's status and standing. Nevertheless, the old lady and her granddaughter who had taken pity on me, or on themselves seeing me in a state of deprivation, did not think like this; they thought it otherwise: in their view, the child should be given some *paise* while going to school so that when other kids spend on such triflings he should also be able to spend and not develop any inferiority complex. In their perspective, in this process, I was developing inferiority complex subconsciously. Now in hindsight I realise that they were perfectly right.

My formidable complexes – mainly inferiority complex -- have their roots in those unbeknown, seemingly insignificant incidents, about which my penury-ridden parents were ignorant and even callous by nature. They were themselves short of money; how could they take care of such finesses of living process, existential necessaries, so significant for the proper development of a child's psyche?

The old lady made it to my house before I could reach there and expressed her anguish at my pathetic situation at not having ice-cream. She also exhorted my parents to invariably give me some money – 'pocket money', as I now have come to know its name – so that I did not develop inferiority complex. The old lady, I think though I am not sure, was possibly a teacher and was utterly sensitive towards such things concerning babies and children. She conveyed this grave message and deficiency on the part of my parents in good faith; nonetheless, that was not my father's stuff; he did not tolerate such good counsels. He took offence to her sane counsel and blandly asked her not to take pity on me in future even if I was sighted standing like a pauper amidst the other school-mates. Rude was his misdemeanour towards the lady; my insolent father was like that only, shorn of all finesses of social and familial life. He behaved usually like a hound and thought that the entire world was set in a fixed frame, never to undergo any change or never to vanish one day.

Later on, when the kind old lady, our distant relative, left, my father, instead of learning any lesson from her sane and sensible counsel, vented her ire on me and my poor innocent mother, as though we had invited her on purpose, to criticise him. I was stunned: instead of feeling ashamed of his inability to meet her monetary duties towards his family and issues, he was calling our bluff; case of a kettle calling a pan black! One who can't meet existential conditions, can't claim oneself to be worthy of begetting babes or issues1

XXX

15. Gol-Gappaas *And My* faux pas

Enter Protagonist

Taking cue from the *icy* episode where I had not shown any initiative to acquire ice-candies despite my other school-mates buying ones, I sharpened my skills somewhat when the other day following in the footsteps of elder school children of our village after the school hours, I reached the bus-stand. I had no option but to follow them: I could not go to my village alone; I was too small by that time to walk alone, on the desolate dust paths from town to the village.

The elder guys at the bus stop ventured to purchase some eatables, *Gol-gappaas,* to be precise. After paying money to the vendor, they started taking the helpings which were one at a time, that is, only after having finished eating the one *gol-gappaa* one could get helping of next one. It was sort of a spicy water filled in an eatable gollop, to be gulped immediately, lest it should break and spill all around. Since I was accompanying them, I thought it was their duty to include me in their eating ventures. By that time I had no idea about the genie of money: that there was something called money which only entitled human beings to partake of anything being sold, or to eat something being offered at shops. I harboured the notion by that time, at that tender age, that whatever was available on the chest of the planet Earth was created by God almighty, not by the creatures living here and, by that logic, everybody was entitled to avail of everything free of cost. Thinking like this, I too stood in the queue and started eating the *Gol-gappaas* along with the students.

The shopkeeper, too, did not suspect my foolishness or childishness. He thought I was part of the group and the group thought I was eating on the strength of money available in my own pocket. They were sensible, I was ignorant as well as foolish and insensible. When the supply chain or the drama of *gollops*

came to an abrupt end, and unsuspectingly earlier than what was expected by the children, they asked the vendor why he had stopped feeding them; he rejoindered, it was already done. Then he included my share too and the realisation dawned upon the elders that I had foolishly partook of their feast. They, however, laughed it off and the shopkeeper rebuked me for a short while if only malignantly; but when he came to learn from the lads that I was the son of so and so teacher – well-known to the vendor too – he too smiled and laughed the matter off. The lads too had pardoned me only because of this fact; to have an influential father entitles one to so many favours in society and everywhere! I was unfazed though I felt embarrassed. However, the vendor exhorted me as if to a thief, "Without money in your pocket, never venture to eat anything anywhere otherwise somebody would beat and berate you badly! There is no free lunch, *Eh!" Adinnaa Daanaa! A la Buddha's* precepts.

I took a lesson for good. For my life! Also, I realised that in the matters of money, every individual is a separate entity; there are no friends, no mates, no family, no father, no mother, no siblings, no relatives, what to speak of shopkeepers and vendors! And that nothing comes for free in the human society. By God's grace, I was spared of the beating and berating, and was let off suffering merely the slightest humiliation; nonetheless, it could not be guaranteed for future *faux pas* or such foolishness if repeated.

This innocent incident became an anecdote in the town and even in my village. Everybody including my father wondered at my foolishness and lack of common-sense. The news had reached my father as well. When he accosted me later, he asked me why I had taken the *Gol-gappaas* without any *paise* in my pocket, I replied plainly, "The other children were eating, I had no money, and since I was accompanying them, I thought, they were duty-bound to include me as well in their eating spree or enterprises!"

The father did not say a second word however! My mother, of course, laughed heartily; it was a childish *faux-pas* worth laughing off, she knew!

I was wondering long thereafter, too, how dangerous it could turn out to be had I not been the son of a teacher!

XXX

10. Unprovoked Thrashing By Urchins

Enter Protagonist

Dogs you might have seen! Whenever a dog comes face to face with another dog, they start growling and fighting with each other or, if there are many, with one another and in the process they hurt and bruise themselves fatally, too, at times.

But dogs are not the only species who exhibit this beastly behaviour: human beings are equally prone to such tendency, of dogs or canines. They too, whenever they come face to face with one another, behave likewise.

I had started to go to the *Aadarsh Paathshaalaa* at the nearby town and was like a pup at that time, hardly six years old or so. Along with me walked to the town school many other children. On the dust-way in between our village and the town there was distance of almost two or so kilometres. But at that tender age it seemed like hundred kilometres and we treading the same at child's pace took very long to reach the school.

On the way, the other children teased me because I looked soft and humble one. One day my most intimate friend by that time was instigated by the children to wrestle with me. He got instigated and without any provocation he started wrestling with me. I could not fathom the rationale of his fighting with me without any provocation. Nonetheless, the life is like that only! People say that the world is governed by the law of cause and effect but my experience has been that the life runs without any logic, it's absurd; no cause and effect tenet works here. Its working is all absurd. The naughty boy was able to thrash me down. I was demoralised at the unexpectedness of the unsavoury incident and the savagery of my mates. I was a bit scared, too, insofar as the human pups were not at all predictable unlike those of the canines.

But God helps those who are innocent and pure of heart. At the nick of the time when I was feeling the insult of being beaten or getting vanquished, my father – that ferocious fellow at domestic front – happened to pass by; he was going to his school where he was posted as a temporary teaching staff. He came to my rescue; he scolded the children for mistreating a humble child like me without any provocation. I thanked God and went away riding the bicycle of my father. Leaving the schoolmates stunned and shocked behind, there.

However, on the way, I think my father was upset that his kind son was being troubled by the vulgar human pups. He kept on enquiring of me whether I was weaker than my mate who had thrashed me to the ground. The matter of fact was that I could not decide whether to fight back or to keep quiet and in this state of ambiguity on my part, and in his childish enthusiasm, my mate conquered me and earned the applause of accompanying savage village urchins.

This incident had its salutary side effects though: my father started keeping watch on me, even as, the accompanying children had got scared of my father after knowing that I was the son of that particular ferocious personage, the teacher; by that time, I think, they were unaware of this material fact concerning me. That way having connections with high and mighty ones does always act as a shield for human species. That is why people always long for having truck with high and mighty. This was true then; this is true even now; this shall remain true forever!

On yet another occasion, the other day, when I was walking back to village from school, one of our uncles who attended the High School at the town happened to pass by riding a bicycle. He saw me staggering towards the village and possibly taking pity on me took me onto his bicycle; and I was very happy. However, in the meantime, my father happened to come by, too. He saw me on the bicycle of my uncle who was my father's younger cousin. My father, for some unknown reason, fretfully forbade my uncle – his cousin – from taking me along on the latter's bicycle. The mystery of which I could not fathom somehow. Now in hindsight I feel that this had something to do with the evil of child abuse – the fucking of innocent babies by paedophiles. My father being a local teacher might be aware as well as conscious of this menace prevalent in Indian rustic milieu and, particularly, in schooling environs. That step on my father's part was sensible, I feel. He could protect his son from child abuse and from fucking in this way.

XXX

17. Boodhe Baaboo Kaa Melaa And My Little Female Guardian

Enter Protagonist

At that tender age too my mother, it seems, was quite liberal in letting me go for outings, of course, in company with the village children: girls and boys. At the town, as an annual function, there used to be organised a local fair – *Melaa* – which was the place for villagers to gather at one place, enjoying the festive atmosphere apart from making purchases of essential items, for at this assembly, various types of items and articles were sold by the shop-keepers, which was not possible otherwise. In the absence of this fair, the poor villagers could not get their items of requirement all at one place.

The *Melaa* was not only a place for shopping and marketing, it was also a judicious spot for match-making which was also so crucial as well as essential a function for society. Otherwise, how to match the young lads and lasses of the area? That's why the atmosphere of the fair is very pleasant, mirthful and romantic. That's why the participants attend the fair in their best attires.

During one such fair, when I heard that on a particular day the fair was to be organised, I insisted with my mother for letting me go to the fair.

"All alone?", my mother interjected.

"Yes, I can go to school; why can't I go to the fair?"

"Going to school and going to the fair are two entirely different aspects.", my mother clarified.

Yet when I kept harping on the same string and created a ruckus in the household, my mother agreed to let me go, but in company with a girl of the village who was of somewhat elder age, but not very much elder to me. She was actually the girl from the *Dheevar* community, those who fetched water to our households: potable water was fetched by servants in our households those days. Hand-pumps or stand-pipes were not yet in vogue.

My mother dressed me in fine fettle and handed me to the safe custody of the little girl. Nonetheless, being a girl from the service class, she was quite pragmatic and active, unlike me who was a perfect duffer being from an upper caste. Both of us reached the fair, even as, there were other kids as well accompanying us from our village. In the village fair, we watched various types of things, spectacles, miracles, swings, toys, shops etc. By the standards of a child, there was too much rush in the fair. The little girl was taking ample care of me for most of the time, but she was only a child, after all. After sometime, when she could not handle me and found her entertainment hindered by my safe-keeping, she asked me to stay under the shade of a tree and commanded me to stay there only, and not to stray anywhere, lest I should be lost in the melee, never to be retraced. On this new dispensation by my little companion, I felt as if I had been betrayed. I thought that she had promised to my mother that she would not leave my finger and would not leave me alone in the fair, whereas now she intended to leave me alone on my own. How should I enjoy the visit of the fair in that eventuality? Anyway, I had no option but to stay put.

She left me alone, on my own under a tree. When I was alone, after some time I started apprehending that if the girl did not come or if in the merriment of the fair she forgot that I was accompanying her and went home, how should I reach my home? My mother was right when she had told me that going to school and going to a fair were two entirely different things, particularly, for a little child like me. Now I realised that I did not know the route to my village. I could see many other people and children from our village in the fair but I thought who would

care for me; the world is selfish! When even my companion had ditched me despite having assured my mother, how could I believe others? In a wilderness, so also, in a *Melaa,* it doesn't matter if one is innocent or little, the beasts prowl and prey upon the softer ones first.

It was when I was thus worried about my eventual whereabouts and my impending loss in the fair that a known lad from our village came unto me seeing me standing there. He offered me to accompany him for seeing the fair. I despite being pleased and rid of my anxiety could not gather courage to leave the spot where my caretaker had left me.

That day I realised how vulnerable a child's life is: wholly dependent on the mercy of grown-ups! The small anatomy of a child is a grave lacuna in the discharge of life's functions! In that sense childhood is a great misery, a grave hell!

Anyway, the girl returned after sometime and fed me something which she had bought for me and I heaved a sigh of relief. To think that I was again restored to safety!

When we reached home, I nevertheless complained to my mother that the girl had left me in the lurch and did not show me everything that was there in the fair. When my mother quizzed the girl, she said that she had left me alone under a tree because it was very crowded in the fair and that I was not feeling comfortable amidst the crowd. That was, of course, true. I felt comfortable standing at a safe distance from the crowd but my remaining alone there was a source of constant anxiety and trauma for me, a child. Still, I am thankful, in hindsight, to my benefactor and little female companion who at least condescended to take me to the first ever fair – sort of human wilderness -- in my life! Nonetheless, a child's, a baby's perspective, was entirely different, widely at variance with that of grown-ups! With that of his companion, particularly! However, unmindful of the considerations of the equally helpless child, the companion!

XXX

Enter Protagonist

When I was in standard 1st or when I was in standard 2nd and even when I was in standard 3rd, I don't know exactly, that is, the years, I had no idea about the concept of years by then. Of course, I had the idea about the place. The village *Paathshaalaa* had been left behind, and I had never thereafter been to that lovely place which was so soothing as well as encouraging to my soul. But my father's idiosyncrasies dictated entirely different conceptions: he did not consider the village *Paathshaalaa* worth the salt and in a feudalistic fervour abhorred it; I too was to follow suit. I nonetheless wondered why instead of going to a school which was so close to my house and where I felt more at home and was able to show my mettle, I was made to go to a town school, to which, I had to commute daily almost two and a half kilometres to and fro, that too, on my two tender feet. Facing all sorts of dangers including that of mistreatment and beating at the hands of village urchins. Also, that school was not to my liking; its vibrations were not good, now I can appraise the ambience of the *Aadarsh Paathshaalaa* thus. For name's sake only it was *Aadarsh* (Ideal) *Paathshaalaa*, however, its teachers did not know how to tackle or behave with small children and how the language of love and affection was more effective than the rule by ruler and the rude and cold demeanour of teachers at that school.

Still, I had little say in such matters. Well, I heard many villagers enquire of my father why I had been withdrawn from the village *Paathshaalaa* and why I had been sent to town school. People also contended that if children from the same village did not patronize the fledgling *paathshaalaa*, how could it develop into a centre of education eventually. I was impressed by the logic of contenders, but my father was made of some different stuff; he didn't care for the overall good of the society, nor was he interested in developing village school into a fledgling educational centre – a *Naalandaa* or a *Taksh-Shilaa*. He was a self-centred sort of person, obsessed with oneself and with one's good. A bit arrogant type of a person too, even as, he responded to the queries of people brusquely instead of responding politely. There was something drastically wrong with the basic structure of his cerebrum and the grey matter ensconced therein.

Whereas our *Paathshaalaa* at village had a fairly sturdy building, the one at town was a ramshackle one; one of its rooms had already imploded, and the rubble was scattered all around. In the remaining two rooms, however, the entire school and its five classes had to be accommodated, with the result that children of different classes all sat together. How the course content was managed for disparate grades by the astute teachers, I can't discover even at this gap of time.

My constant grudge was that I was not admitted to the school formally; I attended the classes though; the catch being that my father used to teach in the High School of that town and had a clout in that small town due to his pedigree – of landlords and influential persons of the area. He had asked the teachers of *Primary Paathshaalaa* to let me attend the classes without having been admitted on regular rolls. I but felt an unease to remain in that state of limbo. Other students were called on the rolls, but I was never called; my name was never called. During those two or three years when I was in the *Paathshaalaa* till standard 3rd, whenever a new teacher happened to join the school, my condition became uncomfortable and uneasy until my father clarified the next day to the new teacher.

In those early days, i.e., in 1962 or 1963, that is, merely 15 years further from the day of partition, the rancour of communalism was still lingering. In the hearts of people! The hearts of even children were full of the hate towards *Muslims* and their innocent children, without any cause, now I realise and rue. I can very well recollect that two lovely and gentle kids of a *Muslim* postman, who was a very nice as well as gifted person, and also, very civilized one, used to study in our *Paathshaalaa*. And the tale I am going to tell is that the other children used to steal their books, note-books, pencils, pen etc. quite regularly, quite frequently, maybe because of this inherent hate towards *Muslims*. The father and mother or the sister of the children were time and time again seen in the school complaining and searching and rummaging through the bags of the other small kids for the stolen items.

That was almost a regular scene. The situation came to an end only when ultimately, getting dejected, the gentle postman withdrew his wards from the school. How pathetic it was! Another consequence of the buffoonery of the 'Father of the Nation' and the 'Uncle of the Nation'! Getting dissected the sacred motherland on the communal lines! Whose bane the innocent kids were destined to suffer! People normally consider the feudal lords and warlords, or even the popular leaders, for that matter, as wise people, whereas the reality is quite the contrary, quite the converse; they are duffers in fact, as their actions on ground, and in hindsight, now reveal.

To be true, we little kids drew sadistic pleasure in the calamity and misery of those *Muslim* innocent creatures and their guardians. How nonsensical indeed! Woe to politics and politicians!

XXX

Enter Protagonist

It was virtually impossible to snatch away freedom from the British, especially, in the aftermath of their victory in the World War II; they were on the sky seventh at that time. Nurturing all along as they were their stooge *Gaandhee*, whom they had made to be called as *Mahaatmaa* with the help of yet another of their well-wisher, *Taigaur*, whom they had patronized and brought to their side by awarding him the Nobel Prize for Literature for a not-so-great piece of poetry, and followed by bestowing a knighthood. Despite having no chances or reason for starting a dialogue for transfer of power to the nationalists, the British started a move to transfer the power, but not to its true claimants, the leader and the soldiers of INA, who had compelled the Britishers by their valiance during World War II and their advances against the British empire, even so, by dint of their resourcefulness in terms of their international reach. The British had realized in no uncertain terms that with the existence of INA on the surface of planet earth and their zeal for combating against the dwindled powers of the British, it was not going to be long in time when the former would be at their throats and would snatch away power through blood-letting, unlike through the sham non-violence that was being prophesied by *Gaandhee* at the behest of the *British Raaj*. All through the World War I, and also, through the World War II, *Gaandhee* was seen busy encouraging his compatriots -- the *satyaagrahees* – to join forces with the Britishers and fight against the enemy forces of their own subjugators. That was proof enough that *Gaandhee* was working at the behest of his masters, the British. All the movements, fasts and campaigns led by *Gaandhee* were calibrated so as to fit into the machinations as well as tactical maneuvers of the rulers at that time.

Given the relentless ferocity of revolutionaries, particularly, in *Bengaals* – both East and West, despite the man-made famine created by Winston Churchill to famish the revolutionaries of *Bengaal,* and in the ghastly process famishing and starving to death the innocent poor in millions, the foreign rulers were finding it almost impossible to survive here. The Indian Civil Servants that came in droves earlier attracted by the charms of Indian landscape, rich culture and luxurious circumstances, now flinched from doing so; the name India aroused a sense of dread in their hearts given the proliferation of violent forces inland, and given the ascent of INA abroad as well as on the fringes of the motherland.

That despite all this the Britons contemplated transfer of power to the natives, that too, without any hue and cry made by the latter, or zeal shown by the latter, so to say, is a great mystery. They were enraged, nonetheless, at the thought of leaving their turf so easily or cheaply, so they thought of making a last ditch effort to exhibit their mite by creating circumstances whereby the compatriots were obliged to think on

the lines that it was better to be in subjugation of foreigners than to be in perennial strife amongst themselves; they created ethnic and communal rift between *Hindoos* and *Musalmaans.* Within *Hindoos,* too, they propagated the divisive theory enunciating that *Sikhs* were a separate race or country. On the caste lines, they had already created thousands of crevices in the society, that is, prehistoric, monolithic Indian society. They had carved the caste system in stone by converting the professions of people as their birth right or more precisely, so to say, their perennial obligations. That treachery helped them rule and exploit the country, however, for almost two centuries, but it destroyed the Indian social fabric irreparably forever. That was a grave *adhammik* or *akushal* act on their part!

The agency – the stooges – they chose for transferring power to natives were none other than those from amongst themselves. Right from *Gaandhee* down to *Nehroo* and *Jinnaah* -- all the three – the trio were but their own men, educated there amongst themselves only; having habits corresponding as well as conforming to their own; having western proclivities as regards culture and convictions *et al.* Throughout the so-called freedom movement, or the Nationalist movement, if you like, they and their press paraphernalia were affording all out publicity and support to these three. They were never hurt in any *laathee*-charge or in any such violent action of forces; others were, the gullible natives were, since the latter thought that their leaders would earn them freedom, and that the latter were getting wounded or bruised, too. It was not so; these three were not scratched even. Of course, they were taken into custody, and it was broadcast with lot of ado and aplomb that they were put in jail. Jail for them was nothing but as luxurious a stay as at their own home, rather, far better than that, for here they were getting everything free of charge and free service of attendants, and free publicity all around the world. That in fact served the interests of the rulers, the Britishers. In this manner, they had at least a foothold in India where they could feel safe and secure – in the name of non-violence, at the behest of an artificially fabricated *mahaatmaa*. Otherwise, on the flip side, there were ruthless and cruel revolutionaries who had no remorse for killing these foreign servants, called their masters.

And the British chose their best chum *Nehroo* for heading the Government of India in lieu thereof. With *Nehroo* at the helms, they were sanguine, it was as good as ruling India themselves, or by proxy, at the worst; instead of a British viceroy, they were having a viceroy whose name sounded native, yet who was more English than any other Englishman, as *Gaandhee* himself had confessed when it was to be decided who would be at the helm of affairs in lieu of the English. The rulers forced *Gaandhee* to accept their *alibi* for transferring power so as to ensure that the power would be transferred only and only when *Nehroo* was chosen as the Prime Minister. They were not willing to transfer power if it was anyone else other than *Nehroo*. And all this was to be arranged in the fashion of a sort of comedietta called Democracy: in the name of Democracy, the *Lok-tantra*. And history is witness that *Gaandhee* sacrificed Democracy for the sake of helping the foreign rulers and, in turn, his protégé, *Nehroo* unashamedly.

In our school, maybe or surely in 1967, we school-going children noticed that a different type of activity was afoot. Various types of people clad in immaculate *khaadee* robes and raiment were seen visiting our town and lecturing people about something new called democracy, the *Prajaa-tantra*. Nowadays nobody uses that term – *Prajaa-tantra* – for *Prajaa* denotes subjects, and in a democracy there ought to be no subjects; albeit the reality is that still all the people are subjects only, except the new species called leaders or VIPs or VVIPs. Those people – some with moustaches and some with beards – looked crazy and their speeches were nothing short of those blabbered by mad men loitering around. Those were not the days of digital communication or the social media, even as, internet was yet unborn. They relied on pamphlets – of small sizes – to advertise their candidacies amongst the public who were mostly illiterate by that time. We, the kids, were fond of collecting the pamphlets of different parties, for there we found printed on them the symbols – party symbols – of them. Now, when I look back, none of those parties is existent; entire scenario has undergone drastic change. Also, the democracy has taken a totally unimaginable turn. There was so much euphoria amongst the public thinking as they were that it were they who were the real rulers, for they had the right to choose their rulers. But was or is that true? They did not realise the cunning of the post-colonial clan of rulers; they were all a class apart. The voters did not have the right or, so to say, the wherewithal to fight the elections themselves, they could simply choose from amongst a privileged few, that is, from amongst a few privileged political families, the *neo* dynasties, mostly family fiefdoms. Despite having demolished the olden day feudal princely states and feudal set-up of *zamindaarees!*

All in the name of Democracy, the *Loktantra,* however!

· XXX

20. My Skull Got Struck In School

Enter Protagonist

At town school, even as I was an utterly shy child, studying in lower classes, not mingling or rambling with anybody, I had to be dependent on other older guys for accompanying them to my village. The village was not very far, hardly two or two and a half kms away, yet for a toddler it was too much; some support even if moral was required, for even a small bestial creature could send him off the track and in the orbit of dizziness.

One day it so happened that I was accompanying my older colleagues – schoolmates – for returning to our village. The school timings were already up, those being the summer days, the days of spring season. The boys were not going straight to the village today; they were haggling amongst themselves regarding certain sports items that had been procured in the school by their teachers, I think, under the subsidy schemes of the then Govt of India. Instead of going to village, they went to the room – hall, rather – where they tried the sports items/ apparatus.

In the process, however, one older sturdy boy tried one heavy wooden sport item that consisted of two heavy and hard wooden balls to be moved around the head quickly. I being a little child could not appraise the risk involved in standing around such lads. In fact I could not guess how large the arms of the lad were, and in the process, when he was moving his arms with wooden balls in his hands frantically, the balls hurt my skull almost fatally. I fell almost faint. The side of my skull went numb. I felt like dying. The blow might turn out to be mortal though. The boys got embarrassed as well as non-plussed, of course, without their ill intentions. They tried to reduce my pain by rubbing my skull with their bigger palms, but the pain was too much for their child's palms.

I got scared that if at the spot of hurt there was a boil or swelling, my mother and father would come to know of it and might scold me for my carelessness, instead of sympathizing with me. I also had the misgiving that the strike might turn out to be permanent and might have damaged some part of my brain for good. Therefore, I decided not to disclose this mishap to my parents, and I didn't. For weeks together thereafter I kept on bearing that pain in the side of my skull all alone and my psyche was down and depressed during that period unbeknown to my parents. In the process, I realized, too, that it was not necessary that the children disclose all the mishaps or abuses taking place with them, and the parents have to be proactive and encouraging to their wards so that the latter do not hide anything untoward

happening to them in the topsy-turvy journey of life.

I do not know whether the violent unintentional strike on my skull damaged it permanently or not, but it certainly proved to be the second almost fatal hurt to my skull after its having been broken open in the wake of falling from the well-head earlier in babyhood in yet another incident.

XXX

21. Sweetness Of Mahuaa & Cruelty Of Human Hearts

Enter Protagonist

From village to the town, there were not only one but two trodden paths. One was the same which I have described heretofore; the other one was from the other side of the village and was somewhat more deserted or isolated, more dangerous too, as per our perception. We children could take any of the routes as per our mood or free choice. Or it depended on the company which I took from school to home; if the children in my company liked the other route, we took the other route. The deciding factor was that the agricultural fields and habitats of those children were on this route, that's why they preferred this route. It made little difference for me whether I took this or that route, for my house was on the farther side of the village from the town and was thus equidistant. Almost!

On one such return journey from school along with some mates I was returning from the other route. The children were not the ones whose fields were on the way; this was a different assortment of school-mates. They were a bit naughty type. Of lower castes, so to say. For me, it mattered little; I simply needed company so as to avert the risk on the way.

When we reached almost midway, my playmates beckoned a *Mahuaa* grove nearby and headed towards that grove. It was the spring season and *Mahuaa* was in full bloom; its flowers having ripened to full sweetness. I was by nature reluctant to accompany them for my mother had forbidden me from taking any diversion from the trodden path. She had commanded me that I should be going in the direction of the tip of the nose and come back in the direction of the nose, straight! Still, because other children were going astray, so to say, I had no option but to follow suit, also because I did not have the courage to tread the remainder of the path myself to village all alone.

I, however, expressed the apprehension that the owner of the trees might be there around or might come and thrash and punish us, but none of the children heeded me. I was quite a small child, maybe I was in standard 1st or 2nd. Quite incapable,

bodily, small-bodied!

The other children climbed the *Mahuaa* trees and started plucking the sweet, ripened blooms and filling their pockets and whatever storage they could think of. They were making noise, too. I was underneath the trees and picking up only a stray flower that had strewn below. I was suspecting that something untoward might happen because the children were indulging in outright theft; theft of someone's harvest.

And lo, while the children were making merry of their exploits of theft – *Mahuaa* theft – the landowner, the owner of the trees sighted us. He was there only, working in his agricultural fields at a short distance. He rushed towards us small creatures menacingly, like a huge daemon, like a monster, with scythe in his hand and using all sorts of obscene invectives against us innocent children. I got terrified, even as, other kids got terrified, too. They jumped off the twigs of the trees and rushed helter-skelter. I too rushed in terrific fear, although I was under the misplaced impression that the adult and grown up man would not do any harm to me because he was well-known to my father and my family, and since he was from our village only. Moreover, I had not stolen anything from his trees. Why should I have been punished then?

The real world, nonetheless, is not that rational. The wonderland of adults and grown up human beings is perfectly irrational and cruel and more beastly than the wild animals are. When I saw him in rage, rushing towards us like the proverbial *Babhruvaahan* or *Angulimaal*, I got panicked and I set off rushing, too. But I was quite near the devil by that time. For him, whosoever was present there was a criminal and deserved death sentence. He threw his scythe towards me menacingly and fatally. Had I not escaped it by the skin of my teeth, I would not be present today to tell you this tale. It escaped me by the width of a thread. I was mortified and stunned to see the meanness of adult world. The grown up humans are not worth trusting; they can be very dangerous, even fatal, for innocent kids. He intended to kill the children. He would not flinch from butchering the kids given the chance.

I somehow managed to escape, huffing and puffing, but I was badly traumatised by this incident – the miscarriage of childish merry-making. The face of that devil and his posture with the fatal scythe in his hand and his throwing the same dangerously towards us has been carved and painted with bloody colours in my heart and mind. I can draw no other image of *Angulimaal* chasing lord *Buddha* other than that of this scoundrel of a farmer.

I remained badly terrified for months together thereafter, but I did not narrate this tale of human meanness to my parents, even as, I was incapable of giving this tale the words. Even now while narrating I have not been able to do full justice to the gravity and ferocity of the incident.

Thereafter, whenever that devil came across me – he did not identify any of us children – I always felt my heart filled with utter hatred towards him and throughout my life I kept on cursing that daemon of a man whole-heartedly. There, while dealing with our family members he was seen behaving very gently. How misleading the demeanours of human beings can be! When it comes to the innocent naughty plays or errands of the children, the adults may be demoniac!

I lost faith in the humaneness of agricultural peasants once again. Despite the intentionally painted or propagated image that peasants and farm community are very kind-hearted or broad-hearted, I have found them always, without exception, quite mean-hearted, wily and cunning. Maybe towards small-bodied, weaklings like kids only! Before the strong, they may feign to be broad-hearted and kind, for there they do not have any other option!

XXX

22. Purchase Of Maize & The Maze Of My Father's Mind

Enter Protagonist

Apart from *Paathshaalaa* which is a place for conditioning the minds of children into social norms through the instrumentality of what they call literacy, i.e.; letters and numbers, there is another place which plays a pivotal role in forming the inner world of the human beings and that is the house of parents.

My father was without exception a daily nuisance for my mother and a terror for us innocent issues of his. We always lived in terror of our father which he himself was least conscious of, deranged as well as insane as he was, though he himself did not acknowledge this empirical fact. He never cared for the agricultural pursuits of the family; he owned fifteen *beeghaas* of very fertile and well-located arable land yet we had never seen him show any concern for his agriculture holding, nor did we children ever have a notion that we were agriculturists. Our cereals did come from the market, not from our land, as we recollect very vividly. We never could associate the land with cereals or foodgrains.

Of those formative days, I have the memory when quite often when the cereals, that is, food in the house was exhausted and it would be the last day of the stock of food in our father's household, our mother did wait with bated breath for the arrival of foodgrains from the market. We were told that our father had gone to yet another town almost six kilometres farther from the town he taught in for purchasing corn; mind you, not wheat but corn, that is maize. How much? Only forty kgs!

For purchasing forty kgs of cereals, that too, a coarse grain like maize, my super-duper, duffer father who was cipher in mathematics, did go to a town almost eight or nine kms away from our village and would incur the transportation expenses along with expenses for transporting the bulk of corn seeds from the town to the village and home! And how much? Merely a mound!

Even at my age of six or seven, I could reason how absurd all this arrangement was, particularly, in respect of the quantity of purchase – 40 kgs – which was hardly enough for 15 to 20 days of diet for such a robust figure as our father. A madman or a fool consumes exceptionally higher quantity of food as compared to the wiser ones!

This situation filled my heart with a sort of inferiority complex thinking that we, despite having 15 *beeghaas* of arable, fertile land of our own, didn't have foodgrains of our own and had to depend on purchase from the market – from 8 kms away – till the last day of exhaustion of the food stock. How pathetic! Or foolish! And it spoke volumes of the quality of a father we had. An unworthy father by all manners!

More agonising was the conundrum that the village being a hub of agricultural activity growing all sorts of foodgrains aplenty in all the households around us – except us individually – why our father could not purchase the same 40 kgs from the villagers or his relatives. Although, in later years, when his misdeeds caught up with him, he was obliged to do the same thing, but that was not through buying but by begging, that is, borrowing foodgrains from the villagers very frequently. And that borrowing was at abnormally and exceptionally high rates of exchange or barter; for instance, for borrowing 40 kgs of foodgrains in the month of December end, he had to promise 60 kgs of foodgrains in return in the month of April next: now, any fool could tell that it was tantamount to an interest rate of 150% per annum. Nevertheless, our arithmetically illiterate father was not aware of such finesses and did suffer ultimately woefully in later life.

I have reached the conclusion in my life from the misadventures of foolishness of my father that a person weak at arithmetic is weak at navigation through the life's stream too. Life is like a mathematical problem and has a definite solution, for reaching which, one has to know and have the exactitude of mathematical processes; mathematics does not have two options or two answers, nor can the answer be reached by trial and error, that is quite a rarity.

Let me disclose, when the small load of maize was unloaded from the cart of the peasant who brought it from the market, that is, town, in his cart in which he had taken his own maize for selling to the same market, did comment on return, "I wonder why *Master* could not buy it straight from here from me; it would have been bought much cheaper!"

But a foolhardy creature has one's own idiosyncrasies, otherwise how would one be differentiated from other sane persons! By resorting to this roundabout mechanism of making purchase from the seventh sky, the *Master* tried to show that his food came from far off, a matter of great pride, *a la,* a '*London returned barrister'* sort of syndrome! In that epoch of post-colonial reign, there was a craze for London-returned things whatsoever!

My mother hailing as she did from a very prosperous and wealthy farming family -- I very vividly observed -- did not feel comfortable on such days; her confidence was obviously shattered and her self-esteem lowered. What could she do but? She was helpless in the face of foolhardiness of her husband! Of the feudal mind-sets of her in-laws!

I thought, however, "Of what use are all these near relatives – these so-called near and dear ones – if they cannot afford us even the foodgrains in our need! These are all sham relationships; there is no substance in them! No near and dear one comes to the rescue of a starving person! One has to starve alone when one does not have foodgrains!"

That childhood impression has continued ever since thereafter and, rather, has been accentuated with the progress of time; and the more astonishing and frustrating feats of my father came to my notice in the coming years.

XXX

Table of Contents

23. An Unworthy Father

Enter Protagonist

Maize apart, for every small provision or necessaries of life, my mother was dependent on the small shop in the alley of our village that was hardly twenty feet away from our homestead. That mother had to send me to that shop quite often for such small purchases as a match-box or some small quantity of jaggery or some other requirement, goes to suggest now to my developed mind that my father did not supply the provisions properly for running the household. The inner reality might be that he did not have money; whatever little or paltry sum he might have got from his High School job where he was an *ad hoc* teaching staff, could

have been squandered off on his habits of showing off amidst his fellow colleagues and on smoking, or on boozing even, most likely. He was in that sort of habit: of showing off and throwing his weight around and telling fake stories to colleagues about his superiority in regard to his caste and pedigree. Apart from that, he was in cahoots with his *Bhaiyaajee* and *Chhotey Daadaa* , both of whom made him to squander money on fulfilling their own demands.

After coming from the school job and having food, he would proceed towards that shop and would recline there on the rope-cot that was permanently lying there for such loafers or idlers who had no other task but to indulge in gossip and loose talks.

Let me clarify, my mother was not authorised to make any purchases from the shop of her own volition; it was strictly prohibited by my father, come what may, let there be no matches or other important provision, for that matter. My foolhardy father had been indoctrinated by village elders, particularly his accomplices – *Bhaiyaajee* and *Chhotey Daadaa* etc - - that the ladies would sell off household foodgrains clandestinely, rather, stealthily for making money. This malpractice was called *'Korchaa'*. And he deeply believed in this story and pretty religiously. And he took all possible steps to check this malpractice verging on fraud of grave proportions! He could not have got the sense of proportion as to what fraud could be made or what amount of corn could be sold off out of a meagre quantity of 40 kgs purchased by him! He lacked sense of proportion as well. And he had great faith in following whatever his wealthy and depraved accomplices would teach him, without distilling it through the sieve or strainer of differentiation between the financial conditions of his own and those of his uncle and *Bhaiyaajee*. The wealthy uncles must be having surplus produce to eat and spare as well as sell too, that's why their lady folks might be making money by this means, and there might be nothing wrong in this in my view, because in the scenario of their men folks not taking care of their requirements, the women folks had every right to sell some share of produce themselves in this manner. But this was a feudal set-up as I have disclosed already, and in such a set-up, it was assumed that the entire wisdom lay in the skull of men folks only, also, that the entire wealth fell to the privileges of men folks only!

One might be thinking that I would be going to the grocery shop for buying something for cash or pies or *paisaa*. No! *Paisaa* was such a valuable coin those days that for us money meant *paisaa* or *paisaa* meant money or wealth. If we intended to allude to some wealthy person, we called one as *'Paisewaalaa'* and that would suffice. But we had no *paisaa* either; we made all the purchases through barter system, by exchanging cereals for the items bought. And in this process, the shopkeeper cheated the gullible villagers at his sweet will. There was no inter-relationship between the price of grains and the price of items purchased. No doubt the shopkeeper feigned to weigh the grains and did some mock calculation in his mind, but now in hindsight I can daresay he did simply pretend to do it insofar as the value of the grains was never more than the value of the item, simply enough! That is proof enough to prove my point.

When my mother used to send me to the shop, she tried to ensure that my father was not present at the shop at the crucial time; and the father was such a scoundrel that he would definitely make his presence felt at the shop at the prime times! At times, to my embarrassment, it so happened that I would reach the shop for purchase of a bit of jaggery – I was very fond of jaggery as all the small kids are – and I would find an unaffable, rascal-faced father very much perched there, gossiping and bantering there reclining on a rope-cot. Both of us got embarrassed in the process, I for having been caught selling grains and father for having failed in ensuring his hegemony on his household in the face of his accomplices present at the shop: that his family was also doing the tricks – *korchaa* -- prevalent amongst lady folks.

After such mishaps there used to be a definite session of riff-raff and shouting at my home – sweet home as they say; it was never a sweet home though! At times father could be at his worst, too, taking liberty even to beat my lovely and kind mother. What a wretch of a husband my mother had got! I used to muse not so infrequently.

I never loved my father, rather, we the siblings never loved our inconsiderate and unaffable father. He was conspicuously irrational and unfatherly, an unworthy father. Not a father, but a male feigning to be our father! A fiend of earlier births to have become our father to avenge against us.

XXX

Table of Contents

24. An Ungrateful Debtor

Enter Protagonist

My father threw up enough hints at his being a deranged skull, and I was able to discern those unseemly tantrums on his part even at the age when I might have been a toddler or not even a teenager. As was his wont, my father did not believe in working with his hands and least of all in earning something by exerting his body or using his skull or skills. He was in the bad habit of begging from one and all. Whosoever one might be! Irrespective of whether one was a youngster or an elder, or whether one was a lady or a lad!

Once it so happened that my father was in need of some money as he ever was. At that juncture in his life he was working as an *ad hoc* teacher at the town's High School. There he was getting a paltry sum as remuneration every month which, too, he was squandering on his profligacies and on his friends. And as a result, he demanded money from my mother as if it was she who was earning money and not him. When my mother could not arrange money as she did not have any at that moment, one teenager girl happened to visit our residence for an errand at that moment. She heard the predicament of my mother as well as father. Being an adolescent, and a girl, she had a soft heart. Resultantly, she took pity, unwisely, on my parents and offered to help them by giving money for a short time, with the hope, and supposing childishly, that my father was a sane and sensible person which he was not.

The pretty girl was none other than the youngest daughter of *Bhaiyaajee*, the same persona whose friend my father was and in whose temperamental and profligate tendencies my father would feel comfortable to be an accomplice. *Sheoraaj* was *Bhaiyaajee*'s son, and the benevolent lass was his sister. They were influential people so much so that they were related to the royal rulers of *Chhaataa – Teekamgarh,* the descendants of *Mahaaraajaa Chhatrasaal.* In fact, the money offered as assistance to my young father was that of his brother *Sheoraaj,* and the same was meant for some specific as well as important purpose. The gullible and innocent girl did not know that she was parting with her brother's money unwittily by handing it over to someone who had no wherewithal to return it in near future, nor had he any such novel intentions to honour the soft feelings of an adolescent girl.

Father was happy on getting the much coveted monetary help in the form of debt, for he never used to care for repayments. He offered a hollow promise to the unsuspecting girl to return the money within a few days.

The few days passed, but there was no repayment of money. The gentle girl gave some concession and benefit of doubt to my father thinking that it sometimes happened that promises could not be kept. And, my father was not the king of *Raghukul,* too! Whose promises could not be broken! Nonetheless, this was not the case; my father had no such qualms of conscience. He minded little if someone of his benefactors was put to hardships due to his breaking his vows.

When two weeks elapsed and my father did not care to arrange and repay the money, it so happened that *Sheoraaj* demanded money from his sister as the cause for which the same was stored had arisen. The poor girl panicked; she rushed to our house and demanded the money back immediately. My father not only could not repay it, but also, did not express any regrets for not repaying, or did not show any gratitude for the support the lass had provided him at crucial time. The girl called all sorts of names to him in turn, even as, she was at receiving end at her own house for her indiscretion in having offered money to an indolent and insolent person none other than my father. *Sheoraaj* had taken her to task for her indiscretion in having lent money to a notorious fellow like my father.

This sort of reprimand, that too, at the hands of a girl was an unknown before as well as unheard of phenomenon for my father. His ego was very high. He was a misogynistic person. He was a foolhardy person. He was a regular wife-basher.

Enraged at this affront of the adolescent girl, even though a benefactor, my father approached someone else equally gullible and borrowed money from there. And rushed to the house of *Sheoraaj* huffing and puffing, that is, to the house of the creditor girl. There he showed his resentment towards the girl in very unseemly manner. Instead of thanking the girl, he rebuked her. That spoke volumes of my father's indiscretion and incivility.

Later on, when *Sheoraaj* came to know of my father's misbehaviour with his sister, as the girl would have narrated her tale of woe to her brother, the latter came to our door and chastised my father offering him sane advice that the demeanour of my father was not becoming of an adult, and that he was venting his ire at an adolescent girl, that too, one who had helped him in his dire needs for money, even by putting on stake his brother's money, simply due to her compassion towards wretches and helpless like my parents. He spoke so many words and in somewhat harsh tones!

My father felt ashamed and mollified a whit.

However, even at that tender age, I was not amused by observing all this sordid drama getting enacted at my home or by my parent. I was angry at my father's misdemeanour. I could realise that he was a man of low esteem and little resources; also, that he was a thankless person with no sense of gratitude towards his benefactors .

In later life, I came across the following exotic verses in *Mahaabhaarat: Udyog Parv,* which enunciate the duties of households:

पृथिव्याम् सागरान्तायाम् द्वाविमौ पुरुषाधमौ।
गृहस्थश्च निरारम्भ: सारम्भश्चैव भिक्षुक: ॥
(समुद्र पर्यन्त इस सारी पृथ्वी में ये दो प्रकार के अधम पुरुष है:- अकर्मण्य गृहस्थ, और कर्मों में लगा हुआ सन्यासी।)

(Meaning thereby, unto the oceans on this vast planet Earth, there are these two wretched persons: an indolent household and an indulgent hermit.)

द्वावेव न विराजेते विपरीतेन कर्मणा।
गृहस्थश्च निरारम्भ: कार्यवांश्चैव भिक्षुक: ॥
(दो ही अपने विपरीत कर्म के कारण शोभा नहीं पाते:- अकर्मण्य गृहस्थ, और प्रपञ्चों में लगा हुआ सन्यासी।)

(Meaning thereby, these two do not behove owing to their paradoxical demeanours: an indolent household and an indulgent hermit.)

XXX

25. *My First Flopped* Ayurvedic *Experiment*

Enter Protagonist

This was inside our compound where cattle were reared and kept; we had a separate arena for the cattle. Around and inside of it there were umpteen number of vegetation and bushes, sort of herbs etc; and we children saw quite often the grown-ups picking some stray vegetation – its roots or leaves – and administer it to someone who was sick. None of our mistake then that we kids mistook every plant or weed growing there as being beneficial to the health of human beings.

One such plant had soft stems, or so to say, twigs which on

being bent could easily be broken, crisply. Amusingly, it also emitted a liquid – sap -- from the end that was broken; it used to be a white liquid, very soothing to watch and touch: and also, to apply on the skin.

Since every plant there was supposed to have medicinal value – being grown in our domesticated compound – I and my cousin, who were sauntering in the compound at that time in our zeal to do something adventurous never done before by anybody, plucked twigs of the soft plants and broke their stems to see the sap ooze out. When the sap started oozing out, we both could not resist the inclination to make use of that milky white fluid: why let anything go waste! We picked the twigs and applied the fluid to our foreheads like a point – a *Bindee* – that our lady folks that we used to see in our households applied to their foreheads. We were very glad that we were ultimately able to discover something by way of applying which as an ink we could write our fates on the foreheads, by writing our own scripts ourselves, putting aside the unseen and unproven Creator whosoever.

And with that new found glory and countenance, with the sap of the poisonous herb applied to our foreheads, we staggered lazily towards our homes like proverbial *Raama* and *Lakshmana*. *Raama* and *Lakshmana* were not alone to walk

around together, there were other pairs too in the world! I and my cousin!

We were expecting warm and glorious welcome by our mothers at home; instead, we got slaps in our faces each one as a first gift, followed by a volley of queries put up by our worried and curious mothers as to where and what and why etc. We too got scared, somewhat. When we told that we had applied the sap of the bush growing in our own cattle compound, the mothers could pacify themselves to a certain extent, even as, they were sure that there was no poisonous plant growing in the cattle compound.

The older ladies – the grandees -- suggested the herbs as remedy to negate the ill-effects of this misadventure of ours and that was administered and to fairly good effect.

Nonetheless, the *phala* – result – of the *kamma* – misdeed -- was to be suffered by us inviolably, inexorably; the scar of the sap applied on the forehead persisted quite a long while on our foreheads reminding us and everybody else that we were the sinners, though ignoramus ones only!

We realised and sort of vowed to our mothers – as they commanded -- that thenceforth we would not eat or apply on our foreheads the contents of any vegetation or plant or bush or herb growing around us, and also, that not all the vegetations and herbs were beneficial for the human body and mind. After experiences gained over millennia the human society has compiled the treatises on medicines – the benign herbs -- and that is enshrined in the form of a *Veda* – compendium of knowledge: *Ayurveda* which is a part of *Atharvaveda*.

Man must adopt the attitude of learning from the experiences of one's ancestors and the entire human race first, instead of experimenting with each and everything on one's own!

XXX

26. Playing Pranks On A Pregnant Lady

Enter Protagonist

Again, like *Raama* and *Lakshmana*, one day, I and my cousin were perched on the upper branches of a *Neem* tree, margosa, in our cattle compound; it was not a compound having any closed boundaries; it was an open space abounding in rich vegetation and tall trees which seemingly were hundreds of years old going by the piths of their trunks. Due to old age or what, like human beings with bent backs or humps in old age, this particular tree was bent at 45 degrees to the earth and posed a benevolent challenge for us young children to climb upon it. It sort of

invited us to climb it – as though to do piggyback riding on its back, like we did on the backs of our fathers.

There was none around; it was evening time, and the sun was about to set; yet my cousin was zealous to enjoy an adventurous climb, even though I was not enthused. I nonetheless followed in the footsteps of my elder.

Even as we were enjoying ourselves gossiping all sorts of tell-tales – true and false -- we sighted a fat lady passing by in that solitude of the compound in the evening. We knew well she was our barber's daughter-in-law, the wife of his younger son. In fact she looked exceptionally fatty to our child eyes and I did not know the reason of her obesity at my age. I simply supposed that the lady was fatty due to eating too much of grains or cereals, more than what she required for survival. But fattiness does not come only because of overeating, there may be other reasons, as I came to realise later on.

My cousin was tad elder to me and he knew many more secrets of the Creation than I did. He sighted the young lady who was supposedly unaware of our presence on the tree. Being on the tree, we assumed that we were hidden from the view when seen from down below, and were unsuspecting and unafraid of any consequences of our misdeeds. Solitude induces one to break the *sheel* (good conduct) and tempts one to profanity easily. My cousin commented, "Here goes a buffalo, you see, and she is *gyaabhan* (pregnant)!"

Being ignoramus, I asked him how he knew about it, to which he rejoindered, "What is there to know about it, she is pregnant; all apparent by the size of her tummy!"

Thereafter, we repeated the insinuation several times in mirth, dead sure in our assumption that since we were not using the word 'lady', instead, we were using the term 'buffalo', we were not offending the lady, least of all, outraging her modesty. We could never assume at that young age that she could take offence to our indirect obscene gibbering from the stem of the obscure tree.

Surprisingly, she did not protest, nor did she show from her immediate demeanour that she had taken offence to our childish reverie. When she passed by and was out of sight, we were dead sure that we had gone scot-free with our criminal as well as mischievous unseemly misdemeanour.

After a while when we reached home, unsuspectingly, we found our mothers enraged. We could not first link their wrath to our misdemeanour shown towards a village lady – our barber's wife, since in our view it was simply nothing – a matter of merry-making or simply a prank. But the lady who was wronged and, in turn, our mothers were not amused; they all took it otherwise. They took cognizance of the lady's grievance made only minutes back. She was just returning her home after having visited our home and having complained, but came back immediately when she saw that we two were coming home.

Our mothers first enquired whether at all we made those profane comments against the lady. We were shocked. How can a grown-up lady make out that we intended to hurt her feelings, though indirectly; and how could she go to the extent of coming our home and complain to our mothers: against two innocent kids? We took the refuge under lies; we uttered, "No, not at all! We were not commenting on her; we were commenting on a buffalo, instead, who was *gyaabhan* (pregnant)!"

"Nonetheless, there was no buffalo around in the compound," averred the lady present there only, having returned.

"We were talking of some other buffalo who was not there but who was pregnant."

The lady vehemently protested it, even as, she was telling the truth.

After some chastising, our mothers realised the triviality of the incident and the childish mirth involved in it; also, the ingenuity of small kids in having applied their wisdom and sense of humour, that too, implicitly. Mockingly, they warned us against repeat of any such misdemeanour verging on profanity in future.

Nevertheless, mirthfully, they took up the issue with the lady who was in some relation to them from the side of her village. They asked her why she must take offence to the remark of the innocent kids, and added that she looked like a pregnant buffalo indeed; if the kids commented likewise what was wrong with that! The lady laughed off, too, the whole episode; and went home smilingly.

However, we were far more educated now: that however implicit or indirect, an offence is an offence, a profanity is a profanity, and it can well be detected by the offended person quite easily. The prevailing circumstances and surroundings of the incident throw up umpteen number of clues to the real intent of the offender.

XXX

27. Jumping The Walls At Dead Of Night

Enter Protagonist

In those days of innocence, I had a time when I used to sleep with my father at the males' residence – *Gher* – probably when my mother had got some other sibling of mine. Father in those days used to be affable towards me. And used to tell me stories. I liked that aspect of my father. Nonetheless, intemperate as he was, when I used to doze or show signs of sleeping, sometimes my father loaded me on his back like a piggyback and ferried me towards the ladies' residence – *Baakhar* -- at late night. For what purpose, I do not know: probably that was the style of males approaching their females in those days of joint family set-up. That was an excuse: to ferry the kid to the females' residence and then stay put there overnight in the company of one's mate.

But my father was my father; he was nonsensical in every respect. At times, when he approached the gate of the *baakhar* – the female residency – the gates were found fastened or latched and my father used to knock at the wooden door first, then stirred up violently the iron chain of the door from outside; and when nothing worked, he would shout like a vulgar urchin at that odd hour of the night shattering the serene silence of the small hamlet. I felt bad about that savage and indecent behaviour of my father, disturbing the sleep of one and all around. Naturally, there was consternation all around at this action of that madcap. Of course, the village folks were conscious that my father was basically a madcap, a deranged person and his behaviour was irrational most of the time.

When the door would not open from the main side, my father would approach the backside of the ramshackle *kutcha* house and would shout from there: that side was nearer my mother's portion and the *kutcha* wall was somewhat lower on that side. There were moments when despite all those tantrums on the part of my mad father the ladies of the house dared not wake up; then my father would jump onto the wall from behind and would make me jump, too, from that rear side to approach the courtyard of the homestead. We thus climbed down to the courtyard from the wall. And reaching the courtyard, he would create very ugly scene, like a beast would, like a deranged person would, that is, entirely unbecoming of the scion of a civilized as well as feudal family. I even at that tender age used to wonder how an adult person of the age of my father could behave indecently without any concern for the inconvenience of the whole neighbourhood at odd hours of the night! Simply to show off and prove that he was *de facto* a mad man!

And one can imagine the plight of my mother and other ladies to some extent when he would reach the figurative battle-field of household courtyard. He would use all sorts of foul language against my mother, by implication involving fucking of her mother *et al.* He was oblivious to the implications of the

tongue he was using at that time. Even at the back of my father perched as I was, I shuddered to think that such an intemperate person could not be trusted as to when he would throw the baby with the bath-tub. Such incidents were not rare; those kept on recurring not infrequently, I presume, whenever need for sensual satisfaction was felt by him. The lady folks too knew this and they did not interfere in the nefarious affairs of this young couple, one of whom was literally mad, and the other one being too meek to protest was suffering her lot in his company.

Not that such incidents were taking place only at my paternal place, that is, my native land; such intriguing episodes kept on taking place even at my maternal place. The other day, for instance, during our stay at *Nanihaal* as usual, and that too during the season of monsoon, when the maize crop and other millet crops were grown in the agricultural fields, and for protecting the maize crop from the poaching birds like parrots *et al* the *machaans* (lofts) were erected in the fields, and perching on them the households tried to shoo away the poaching birds, we being at our *Naanaa's* house particularly during that season felt abnormally gay because the Nature at that juncture presented such an exotic view all around and it seemed so mysterious as well as other-worldly! And to add an icing on the cake as it were there was the prospect of sitting on the loft, particularly during morning and evening hours, when its pleasure multiplied manifold. The coolness of weather coupled with the incidental downpour of rains if at all made the atmosphere so salubrious!

Nevertheless, the one off incident I am going to narrate here pertains not to the morning or evening hours but to the noon. On the loft we were three children; me, my maternal cousin *Surendradaa* and yet another lad – of course, also a near relative cousin – *Vinod,* and we were discharging our duties of guarding against the onslaught of birds, the poaching birds, possibly sincerely. The loft was in fact erected taking the support of a *babool* (acacia) tree, on the joint of two branches of which, one edge of the loft in the shape of a rope cot was fitted and to support the other edge of the cot two wooden logs were erected crossing each other and forming a joint at the meeting point just emulating that of the acacia tree. It was tied tightly and there was no risk of it coming crashing down at all. The consideration behind this tightening of the loft was that we the children or even other children, for that matter, would not mind jumping and hopping on the make-shift loft unmindful of its fragility. And the incidents of lofts coming down crashing were not far and few between, too!

We the three children were exactly in that category, and we had been sent by our elders there as a replacement for the elders who had gone to the village for finishing their daily routines and other chores, like, taking of bath and for having lunch *et al.* For they knew that the birds had also gone to take their lunch at their homes, their nests! Albeit the family elders did not have much of a faith in our collective sincerity! Rather, the converse would be true when we three were together!

And we were not guarding against the birds; rather, we were making merry at the loft. For instance, we noticed that there was a nest of some bird on the upper twigs of the acacia tree just above our head. The poor helpless creature would never have suspected while making her nest there in fond hope of laying eggs and hatching them there that the ever greedy humans would encroach upon her only preserve at the twigs of the lofty tree swaying in the blue sky! But the man had done that only! Unmindful of or unconcerned about the well-being of the poor little creature and its impending issues, the fledglings!

Incidentally, we three also observed that one of the fledglings of the bird had fallen off the lofty nest onto the ground and was crying there piteously opening its beak and lay on its back helplessly. How it could have happened! When we had arrived at the spot of the loft, the fledgling was not there on the swampy ground. That mishap might have occurred as a result of our childish merrymaking tactics as well as antics whereby the young as well as soft branches of the tree might have swayed violently making the helpless fledgling to fall down.

We being the children did not realize the gravity of the situation and, rather, started despising the ugly spectacle presented by the fallen creature's anatomy. We could never even imagine in our thoughts that it was our duty to pick up the helpless baby bird and put it back in its nest. No such compassionate actions – *dhaammik kushal karmas* -- had ever been taught to us by our parents; rather, in our myopic views we did not think that any other creature other than the human beings deserved any pathos from us humans! The pathetic scene continued for some time and then became silent; the creature had died.

However, when after some time someone came to the loft for relieving us from our childish insincere duty, he or she reproached us for the insensitivity shown by us towards the fellow *satva* that the fledgling was, however, in another shape. We were however least bothered being the kids.

When we reached home, the denouement was there at hand as if ready at hand! My mother being the most active and dominant member of her maternal family called us and asked us what we were indulged in at the loft. She implied we were indulged in something slimy on the loft, that is, we were doing something verging on sexual misdemeanour. When we genuinely expressed our ignorance about what she meant by indulging in objectionable activities at the loft, my mother shouted to all of us saying that we were lying. At this outrageous accusation we three got enraged and we three protested vehemently against the false allegation. The fact of the matter is that the loft and the field where we were perched was not very far from our *Naanaa's* home; it was rather quite in straight view of the roof of the house which could be seen by any healthy and sharp eye. Why only sharp eye; even it could be ascribed any notions as per one's own volition, as did happen in this case, whereby we children were accused of getting indulged in doing nothing but obscene activity.

After some haggling, albeit to my mother's disbelief, we were acquitted of the charge of fucking one another on the loft, with the intervention of our younger *maamee*, who virtually reproached my mother that she was casting aspersions on innocent youngsters colouring their activities with her own coloured viewpoint. Whatever one thinks, one perceives actions of others in the same light, she added. With this intervention, our opinion about *Maamee* improved tremendously whereas that of my mother got tarnished equally proportionately. Nonetheless, I set off wondering how to guard against such slimy accusations as this one during our childhood, when we are innocent, and also, ignorant; yet any one crooked could make use of our innocence and defile our bodies and prestige. Also, how to keep from the harm's way as regards the sexual misdemeanours of the grown-ups who seemed to be ever on the prowl. Throughout my babyhood and childhood that however remained a big issue with my innocent psyche: that I might be downright righteous but any one treacherous could play havoc with a child's impeccable life and body!

The anatomies of all the living beings – the *satvas* – are nothing but the sexual devices.

XXX

28. *Curses Of A Child Never Go Waste!*

Enter Protagonist

The timings were those of morning: we were preparing to go to school, I to my *Paathshaalaa*, and father to his teaching job – *ad hoc* one. There was no such thing or a hint as an oncoming storm in the household, although the storm could arise at any time for which we always feared; our father as a species was ever unpredictable. He was actually a boozer at that time: a snake in its prime and slough, oblivious to the realities and travails of life. I had not yet had food. Mother was preparing for cooking the food.

Suddenly, I saw father asking my mother for some money; he was in the habit of demanding money from the mother like shameless urchin whenever he would have squandered his salary on dissipation and intoxicants.

I wondered how my mother could arrange money for this insolent and irrational creature of a male. My mother tried to keep some rupees spared for emergency, like health and the like, that too, out of the money she received from his parents as presents when she used to visit them – and she visited them quite frequently for this aim specifically at the back of her mind.

Mother feigned lack of money and told him that she didn't have any money that day and that she had already parted with whatever little she had in her possession. However, the insolent husband was not to accept this statement; he was of the opinion that whenever he demanded money for floundering, his wife must needs fork out from her purse some money out of some feat of wizardry. Such a rogue actually he was!

When mother tried to reason with him and gave an account of the help she had provided on such and such dates and that she no longer got money from her parents that much, of late, since the latter had come to realise, too, that theirs was a bottomless pit or pot – my father's, that is – they had realised the futility of wasting their money, and rightly so. There is no use spending money on a buffoon, an indolent creature!

When mother did so, the chauvinist male lost his temper – temper anyway he would lose at the slightest excuse; he considered himself an immortal being, never to die or perish, it seemed by his behaviour – and he started beating my mother in front of me – a small kid, helpless and hapless, given his little bodily prowess – child's. The male monster got in such a rage that he picked up a thick wooden log and beat my mother as a savage person would beat a beast, without little concern where it was falling on the fragile human body of a fair sex. Such a daemon he was! I thought! *De facto* a fiend, an apparition!

I could not even afford to weep. I could only vow at that juncture in my heart that when I would grow up I would beat this beast of a human being like this only. His beastliness was so apparent and abhorrent for me!

However, to my amazement and chagrin, in that sprawling courtyard abounding in so many so-called 'near and dear ones', that is, blood relations, nobody ventured to come to the rescue of my beloved, lovely and gentle mother. I formed a very bad opinion about them all, as well. No relative is of any use for a beleaguered person; all relations are sham, I concluded even at that tender age that is supposed to be having no wisdom of one's own.

My mother's bones were cracked, the beatings had marks of swelling on her entire body. What to speak of her self-esteem and honour among her peer level ladies! The old grandees were pleased to see that a male was wielding stick on the back of a female folk. A lady is always a born enemy of women folks! Ladies, especially, aged ones do feel glad to see such masculine tyranny being shown towards their juniors – junior females, I don't know under what programming of grey matter by the Creator of this universe!

I could not think at that tender age that in such a situation how the things would turn out, that is, how I would go to school, how the food would be cooked etc. I thought the mother would still cook the food despite so much hurt, humiliation and bruises on her body. It was not to be. I decided not to go to school and sympathised with my mother instead. But to my chagrin, the beast got ready for his school - without having food -- food he did not deserve anymore after this bestial misdemeanour -- he rather deserved fodder fit for cattle – and he commanded me to accompany him to school. Without food, without my lunch! A child to school, without having food! He was so inconsiderate, rather a duffer! Food he could never afford us even in his later life!

I wondered how after having created so much violence in the household he could ask me to go to school, to a child whose mother was beaten before his baby eyes by him! How could a child balance one's psyche in such circumstances! How could a child bring oneself psychologically to go to school or for studying in the school. I wondered! But the beast did not wonder. I, however, wished in my heart that if my father were dead that day how pleased we would have been! How lucky we would have been! All of his blood relations! But that wish was not to be fulfilled; father, that beastly persona, lived full length, with almost the same bestiality throughout, long thereafter!

I had no option but to follow suit. I feared that if I refused he could beat me as well with that thick log. A beast could not be trusted; in rage he could do anything – one who could beat his wife so cruelly!

I was morose extremely and was throwing all sorts of curses towards that beast, throughout the way from my home to my school, cursing: 'May God my father die! May God my father's job be lost! May God my father's arrogance be subdued and he be mellowed! May God my father be punished divinely and be taught a lesson befittingly!'

I can still recall after almost six decades' gap that throughout the way I was contemplating or praying like this to something or someone called God. By that time, I had unflinching faith in the concept of something or someone called God, although in later life, I have come to realise that the entire phenomenon of Cosmos is nothing but God and whatever we utter or do or wish is nothing but the desire of God only and, if effective enough on the strength of purity that is truth, is fulfilled too, materialised too.

I reached school. On the way, my father asked me, as though he did not know, whether I had had food. How could I? I responded angrily, "*Kahaan tey*? (How could I?)". To which he rejoindered nonsensically as well as insensitively as was his wont. I was wondering how I would survive the day without food. I could not even imagine that man does not die without food for one or two days, rather, one feels good and much better by not having food for one or two days; that this voluntary pursuit of giving up food is called fast. But father had no qualms about my not having had food. He was such an insensitive male!

I reached school but my mind was constantly with my mother – weeping and crying without tears. I feigned to play with kids but without my mind being there in the school. How much we feign to be happy amidst our mates whereas the reality would be entirely contrary! We are obliged to respect our hateful parents, whereas in heart we wish them all the worst and all the hell! I was doing nothing in the school that day but only wishing that my father be dead and that we be ridden of his existence and connection with us in our life.

In the evening I returned home – shamefaced, feeling as if I had beaten my mother myself; I could not see eye to eye with my mother. My mother asked me why I did not protest when that beast of a father was beating her and why I did not ask about her condition while going to school. I had no reply; I could not think or contemplate on those lines, I didn't have that faculty; I was not trained or groomed like that; such virtues do not develop of their own, those have to be taught to the children. I was not. Mother was still not well; her body was aching everywhere. More than the body, the hurt was mental and moral, and also, to her self-esteem.

She reasoned with me as to from where she could produce money when she didn't have any? I realised it fully but her devilish

husband did not! Her indolent and insolent husband despite himself being good for nothing and incapable of earning a *pie* expected others, especially her wife, to produce money for him, figuratively, to hatch money for him like eggs. He was such a duffer! There onward, I had no such feeling towards my father that he was my father; I took it as if a deranged and insane male lived in our household feigning to be the husband of my mother and having sex with her forcibly and begetting babies only, without any concern for their upbringing or career or sentiments.

In the evening the beast returned, too, without any remorse, without any compunction and sat down to have his food, to fill his belly unashamedly; the same food cooked by the hands of his bruised and unwell wife! How shameless is the world of relationships in human society! Even between husband and wife! I felt so palpably.

Of course, father did not die untimely death despite my fervent appeals to God; nonetheless, his job was gone in near future, his arrogance was shattered and he mellowed down eventually; he became a pauper, a beggar virtually, he lived on borrowed money – borrowed at sky-high rates – which he could never repay and which were repaid by me in later life; his house crashed in rains whereafter he could never have a house of his own till his death – he stayed in the house of his elder brother thereafter, etc. And that shelter also eventually got cracks in the walls! As a consequence of his stay therein as though!

I think this much wretchedness was becoming of his sins – his misdeeds -- apparent sins and crimes. In hindsight now I realise that the curses thrown by children and babies never go waste; they materialise as such. Father lived long for he had to endure all those miseries befalling him as a fallout of a child's curses. Even during later life when I was not a kid, my father was not a reformed person; his tantrums persisted unabated, almost like that only, with only slight modifications due to incapability of age in that he could not wield the stick or log on the back of my slender and tender mother, his wife!

XXX

29. *Wilderness Of Literacy*

Enter Protagonist

They say the world of literacy resembles a wonderland, full of miraculous revelations emerging day by day. Indeed it must be as the name suggests, first miracle being that the spoken speech is symbolised, that is, converted into symbols: and there is no set or single way to do that; there are millions of methods to transcribe the spoken speech into symbolic shapes throughout the world. By that score, even the vocal speeches are millions throughout the world. Innumerable! Rather, every individual being uses one's own unique tongue.

However, seen minutely, at an inner level, it gives the impression that wonderland it might be but this is more of a wilderness, a wild world. All manner of wild activities do take place in these so-called pious institutions of learning, where both letters, that is, alphabet, and numbers, that is, mathematics, are taught. To begin with! Though at later stages, stretching the instruction too far they start feeding all manner of rubbish into the formative minds of ingenuous children. They claim to be embellishing the brains of grown up guys, but the experience of human society suggests that higher education merely goes to defile the human brains; deforms its natural shape!

Our father was one such glaring example of the fallouts of said wilderness: he was wild towards not only his wife and issues, but also, towards, his pupils, that is, students at the High School. There used to be many complaints made by the beaten kids to their parents but the pedigree of this wild man came to his rescue; the parents of harassed students did not take any harsh action against my father, like manhandling of him, as they usually would have done in case of other not-so-pedigreed teachers.

Beating of teachers at the hands of parents, guardians or grown-up students was not a rarity even in those supposedly savage days; such instances kept on seeping through the grapevine incessantly. It's not a speciality of only the modern times when culture has been spoilt completely.

At our *Paathshaalaa* itself, we had very queer characters in the shape of teachers. One such teacher was our head master – '*Raajpaal Maassaab*', as we called him dreadfully. His voice had a high baritone and very high pitch. He did not seem to have spoken a sweet language towards any student throughout his life. He always spoke abnormally aloud and at a very high pitch. Even if he did not beat a child, mere his shouting was terrifying enough for the students, to make one urinate in the *pyzaamaas*, more dreadful than physical beating. We the students shuddered at his sight. The commands of *Raajpaal Maassaab* were inviolable like those of the Nature whose laws can't be broken. Nonetheless, the teaching effectiveness of this head master was very high; he was considered to be a very intelligent teacher and his students always excelled in the subjects he taught, e.g. arithmetic. Fear psychosis is such a double-edged sword which can cut the leniency finely away from the industriousness.

Another such teacher was '*Bhaagad Bhoot*' as we children called him in private. He was a very tall personality, of a martial race and his voice was loud, too. But he did not sound as ferocious as *Raajpaal Maassaab* did. His demeanour was kind sometimes whereas that of *Raajpaal Maassaab* was infallibly harsh always. *Bhaagad Bhoot* believed in natural living, in nature cure, and was seen reading literature of naturopathy in the school, and also, suggesting to students the natural remedies for curing themselves of the trivial ailments of day to day. Despite his fearsome countenance, we were sure, *Bhaagad Bhoot* would not do us any physical harm. We observed him walking towards his village with very long strides, on foot, that's why children started calling him '*Bhaagad Bhoot*', implying a rushing phantom.

In narrating these two memorable figures from my initial schooling my intention is not to decry or demean those noble souls at all, who are no more in the frame of existence on this planet presently; nor will they ever be now, at least in the same form; in any other form or shape they however may be present! The frame of existence is ever changing without a break! I have simply reminisced them, since they were instrumental in moulding our brains, thinking and characters indelibly and inexorably. However, that artificial façade or speech or behaviour towards little children was the necessity as I now realise in hindsight. The little children can't be disciplined except by mock strictness and that is necessary. It's like moulding an earthen or metallic pot by beating it with some hard stick or such other thing; only then the pot takes its desired shape. Rather, a metallic pot takes fire to soften it so as to accord it the desired shape!

If at all there were such characters as those two teachers, there were also teachers who were very affable and kind-hearted towards little children; they could never utter a harsh word. One such teacher we loved so much, and on his transfer suddenly to some other place following his tiff with *Raajpaal Maassaab*, we students missed him dearly. The fact was that in our class, he used to tell us the stories of *Mahaabhaarata* and *Raamaayana* and we kids were mesmerised so much by the miraculous incidents taking place there in those stories! The style of story-telling of this teacher was so sweet and enchanting that children kept sitting for hours, particularly, in rainy seasons when it was raining cats and dogs outside; it was a treat to listen to this teacher telling us tales of *Mahaabhaarata* and *Raamaayana*. His conviction was that the characters of children might be moulded by telling them classic stories; and by means of these classics they could get the lessons in the art of living. And we

did agree with him; those sessions were not boring at all, whereas all other sessions used to be unbearable and tortuous for us kids.

But our strict *Raajpaal Maassaab* had different opinion in this regard; he used to believe in following the rule book and in not deviating from that at all. He believed in traditionalism, in conventionalism, like *braahmans*, even as, he was one. His point seemed to be off the mark. Human society and the world is undergoing change incessantly and the norms set by any one particular person – be one a sage or a legal luminary or an educationist – cannot remain valid and applicable for good. They warrant continuous revamping to conform to the evolution of the world.

At school, though I had command over alphabet and letters, I didn't get a handle at numbers at all. That bizarre world of numbers did seem to me like the wizardry of the sorcerer who used to come to our village showing his magical tricks which, too, we could never fathom. I could count numbers and recite them too, but beyond that when they entered the realm of commutation and permutation of numbers in the name of addition, subtraction, division, multiplication, *et al*, it became an intractable maze for us children, nay, not for children, for me only. However, sharp I was in linguistics, I was a perfect duffer in arithmetic at that time. With the result that I did not command any respect or place among the fellow classmates or schoolmates. As though as an icing on the cake was the peculiar status of mine in school whereby I was not a regular student of the school. I was attending it simply at the mercy of teachers and as a result of the clout of my father in the town and on the primary school teachers. Well, that much effectiveness and goodwill my father, of course, commanded in the outside world, in the world outside the precincts of his own household. His image inside the household and that in the outside world were entirely at wide divergence! In domestic circles he was a crazy, incurable guy, whereas in unknown circles – for those who did not know him intimately – he was a hero, a leader, a dynamic personality, and ironically, an affable personage. At school and in the town where the school was situated!

His stature had got an unprecedented boost with the visit of *Naaib Saahib* since in those days *Naaib Tehsildaar* was taken by simple villagers to be a greater post than even *Tehsildaar* given the illiteracy and gullibility of the country folks. Because an additional word – prefix -- '*Naaib*' was there, and *Tehsildaar* had no such '*Naaib*' attached to that! By the norm of 'the more the better'!

Literacy and illiteracy can both be equally relishing and entertaining pursuits! Like, there is no single law of the jungle -- some animals are cruel and some are kind -- there is no single concept regarding schooling as well: some teachers contend that love and affection are a preferable mode to teach or instruct the children, whilst there are other set of teachers – and they are aplenty, rather, in majority -- who claim that 'spare the rod, spoil the child!' Just like in a wilderness!

XXX

30. Jungle Jaanaa *(Going For Nature's Call)*

Enter Protagonist

Schooling renders human species indolent and insolent without affording any substance: this modern education! Albeit my grandfather did not turn wild as a result of his pioneering schooling, he had definitely developed the vice of indolence and sham superiority. An aversion for work by hands, that is, physical labour! His elders had sent him to school, first at a nearby town, then to *B R College, Aagaraa*, in the fond hope that their progeny would become something special, but on the contrary, both of them – the cousins – turned out to be worse entities: one died of consumption, that is, *TB*; the other one lost his basic faculties for living, or for how to arrange the wherewithal for earning a living, that is, basic necessaries of life: *rotee, kapdaa* and *makaan*!

The elders of the broad family tree nevertheless did not learn any lesson from the spoiling of two youths of first generation of 'schooling', and they kept on sending children to schools instead, to what purpose, I can't fathom. Well, by that time, of course, one more feather had been added to the so-called spectacle of education, and that was that a schooled child could earn a bigger dowry in the marriage market. People developed a false notion that educated children would get a job definitely, for such stock of educated youths was very limited. Dowry no doubt was a prestigious social evil even at that time as were all other social evils inherited down the millennia in our society.

My father too reached the school, and also, the college, and crossed that perceivable bar called Graduation which was the highest mark of literacy in those days. Nonetheless, all the convictions proved to be false when it came to my father's career: he did get a sumptuous dowry in child marriage but didn't get a job, however. Not only then, but even later; never! One can harness an ass however magnificently, yet its outcome would ever be the same: that of a donkey! Of what avail was the graduation then? To what good? You can't convert a donkey into a horse!

Our mother's sojourns between her in-laws and her father's house were very frequent as I have mentioned earlier, too. Due to my father's habit of shirking his marital responsibilities! He sort of could not reconcile to his child marriage and the devastation of his mental landscape ever since. Already his brain was cracked since the wailing at the time of his mother's untimely demise; now his career had been cut short, too, by the rusticity of his family elders; his demi-literate father remaining a dumb spectator, a naught throughout all those activities, sort of spoilsports on his part. That's why I tend to contend as to what the use of all this modern education is! It merely goes to mar the innate initiative of a person and whatever natural guts one has, to face the life. It makes one dumb and deaf! And entirely incapable of handling the phenomenon called life!

On one such return journey from our *Nanihaal* to our paternal village, I along with my mother first waited in the *Dharmshaalaa* for quite long. Then after a long wait, our grandfather appeared at the scene with a bullock-cart which he had obviously borrowed from some wealthy and resourceful villager, for in our household we didn't own any bullock-cart. This lack of resources – even so trifle a thing as bullock-cart – filled my child's heart with lot of despondency and inferiority complex, and also, wonderment inasmuch as on the one hand, they claimed to be the best family, greatest family, of not only the village, but also, of the area (and the world!), and on the other hand, they did not even have a bullock-cart despite living in a village, even as, they were pursuing the profession of agriculture and needing carts to ferry the crops and hay from fields to barn to home! However, the final denouement is that they did not possess a bullock-cart! My grandpa came with the cart and we boarded it in a melancholy mood, with not much of a zeal, coming as we did from the Elysium of our maternal grandfather's home.

On the way, rather throughout the way – from the *Dharmshaalaa* at the town to our village and home – I overheard my father arguing and quarrelling with his father nefariously and in a very profane mood. We – me and my mother – were wondering why on a day when his wife and issues had returned from his in-laws', he instead of being pleased and merry was all rage and upset. The reason was that he was upset exactly for this reason; why they, that is, we, had come back! He had a life-long grudge against his father that he did not intervene when his career was being butchered by way of child marriage and let him be made a slave to dire straits. His

arguments and tussle stopped only when we had entered the precincts of the hamlet. Let me as a child be very clear that I made a very bad opinion about my father at that time, even as, I used to keep on hearing all sorts of adversarial remarks against my father in my *Nanihaal* from the mouths of one and all, without exception. They would all be ruing the day when they had married their daughter or sister with such a worthless urchin of a sham feudal family! So, in case of my father, the schooling and modern education had turned him apparently wild. Instead of making him a sensible and civilised human species!

Nonetheless, wild animals amongst human shapes abound in our society. If my father was the villain on paternal side, my maternal uncle – *Maamaajee* – was a much ferocious villain on maternal side. In my childhood or babyhood I harboured the fear psychosis that if I felt natural instinct to go to toilet at night, my *Maamaajee* would be enraged. Everybody was supposed to go to *jungle (*toilet) only during day time - - fixed timing. Easing one of natural requirements was called going to *jungle (jungle firne jaanaa)*. Everybody had to go to the fields for easing off/ excreting. We children had no command over this natural tendency and tried our best to check the excreta inside our intestines, come what may, during night time! Imagine, how vulgar a society it would have been! Although there was no such ban or pronouncement from our *Maamaajee* that no one would go to jungle at night, we owing to his unaffectionate as well as unpredictable demeanour had deduced in our minds that he would chastise us if we went to *jungle* at night.

At times when it became intolerable and when I felt that it might seep out and spoil my underwear, I felt constrained to summon my mother in horrified and scary voice, "*Beebee, Tattee lag rahee hai*! (Mother, I am feeling like going to loo!)" and suspected that my mother would rebuke me, too, for this untimely indenture. But my mother was a kind-hearted and sensible or seasoned lady who knew that natural tendencies had to be honoured lest they should result in incorrigible damage to the innards of a living being; she would respond invariably with a kindly response, "Ok, no problem! Come on!"

And we – mother and her little son – would walk from the inner portion of the sprawling house to the outer portion where *Naanaajee* and *Maamaajee* used to sleep and live, and from there to the adjacent agricultural fields. On reaching the fields, I felt so much relieved indeed! There is no greater relief than easing off the natural instincts!

Our *Maamaajee,* and also, *Naanaajee* sometimes hemmed and

coughed deliberately on such occasions so as to let us know, and to give us courage at night, that they were awake and that we needed not worry. I, however, wondered at the temerity of my mother in my childish thoughts that my mother was not at all scared going out in the night. I considered my mother very brave and bold at that time.

But the same courageous lady: how timid and tamed she had been made by my wild and vulgar father in the wilderness of his feudal set-up and wilds of his fake schooling which had given him naught and had, rather, made no value addition at all! His schooling had rather snatched away from him the natural humaneness that he might have imbibed had he remained an unschooled, illiterate and uneducated being!

I observed all around me multitudes of unlettered and illiterate or uneducated folks – village folks – who behaved more civilly and more humanely than our so-called 'educated' father did. Not only behaviour-wise, the latter were more adept at handling the issues of life than my so-called 'educated' father and grandfather were.

XXX

31. The Most Intractable Problem Of The World

Enter Protagonist

I was good at language, yet the numbers I could not fathom at all. It was alright till it entailed merely the counting of numbers. As soon as it entered the arena of other magics of arithmetic, I was a perfect cipher; I could not fathom anything. And this condition continued till standard three. One day, my teacher asked the students to do the sum of 'one plus one'. On hearing the teacher, the students became very happy and got busy in doing the sum and did it within no time. I could not comprehend anything what it all meant. I had never heard about addition. My father himself was cipher in mathematics. The boys were all happy and gay and were enthused to show their solutions to the teacher. I was the only one who could not do this sum: supposedly the simplest sum of the arithmetic. I simply wrote one on my slate with the slate pencil and kept sitting, dumbfounded, bewildered as to what to do!

The students, when they came to know that I had not done one plus one, and that I did not know how to do it, were baffled, too, equally: how come a student of grade three could not do even a sum of 'one plus one'! Could not add one with one! Quite strange indeed! What sort of a duffer this boy was! The teacher was also baffled: what was there in this sum, the simplest question of arithmetic! The simplest sum of the universe, of the Cosmos, possibly! He made his face in vexation. But did not venture to tell me the secret of solving this seemingly simplest sum or the simplest problem of the Creation, the Nature. The boys readily got a dummy to make fun of. They had not seen such a buffoon in their lifetimes yet as though!

I felt so perturbed and shattered to think as to what my fault was! I had never been taught how to do the sums or other aspects of arithmetic, for that matter. That was the day of gravest humiliation for me in my life ever.

Crestfallen, I came home. My sensitive and beloved mother immediately got the scent of something wrong with my mood. I told her that I had been humiliated in school because I could not do the sum of 'one plus one'. I was confident that my mother would be knowing how to do the sum of 'one plus one'. However, my mother expressed ignorance about anything to do with arithmetic; even 'one plus one' she could not do! In fact she did not know the implication of the word 'addition'. I felt doubly crestfallen. Now, who would guide me to come out of all that ignominy. That was only the beginning: tougher sums were there on the way; how would I solve those if I didn't know how to do even 'one plus one'!

I had no hope from my insolent father. I did not know that despite being a graduate, he was duffer and cipher in mathematics, too. Even if he did know, I was sure, he would not guide me, rather, I apprehended that on my asking him to guide me he would choose to rebuke me.

Still, when in the evening he returned from the school and had had his food and was in a comparatively normal mood, I sitting on my rope-cot with a granite slate in my hand and with a slate pencil, ventured hesitantly to ask him, "*Pitaajee!* How to do the sum of 'one plus one'?"

On hearing this, the gravest of pieces of information as though in his entire life, he startled and thumped his forehead with his palm adding morosely, "*Ah*, you don't know even this? What an ill-luck?" Yet, he did not condescend to explain the problem to me and to solve the same. In the process, I felt deeply disheartened, although I had never expected my father to guide me as was his general mien, that is, always self-centred, self-indulgent ever.

With both the citadels of hope and recourse having collapsed one by one within short span of half an hour, I was left in the lurch, with the prospects of further humiliation at the hands of fellow students and teachers at school. This prospect traumatised me horrifically. What to do now?

I sat on my cot as if I were the lone survivor of the Cataclysm, of the Apocalypse, alike the proverbial *Manu* of *Kaamaayanee* epic of *Jay Shankar Prasad*; as though everything had been devastated and nothing was left intact in the entire Creation except me: I was my own guide as though! I was my own island as though! As the *Buddha* said: *Appa Dweepo Bhav!* (Be your own island!) I was on my own!

What to do now? My mother was sorrowful, too, to see me – her pupil of eyes -- morose and not being herself able to help me out of this despondency. She suggested me to consult someone else: there were so many others around in our wider family circle. But I had lost all faith in the relationships, least of all, in their wisdom: when my teacher did not guide me, my classmates did not guide me, my mother could not guide me, my father did not guide me, instead the latter even chided me, my classmates made a fun of me and called me the worst duffer of the Creation, I was unwilling to take any further humiliation, any further risk of heart-break.

I kept sitting in that posture for quite a while. Nonetheless, as they say, 'adversity is the mother of invention', and also, that 'every question of mathematics has a definite solution', I ultimately got wearied of my wretched state of mind and mood. I wrote 'one' in numerals on the handy granite piece of slate. Again I wrote 'one' on the same handy granite piece of slate. Twice. The 'one' had been uttered by the teacher. Then I made a sign of addition in between those two 'ones'. The issue though had been transcribed into symbols but to no end, to no avail yet! Further course of action was not known, nor was there anybody around to educate me out of this *Chakravyooh a la Abhimanyu* of *Mahaabhaarata* repute, or *a la Alee Baabaa* of 'Arabian Nights' repute, who did not know the code word – the sesame -- for opening the door to the treasure trove of forty thieves!

Suddenly, all at once, someone spoke from within me: what's 'One'? In terms of fingers?

I raised one finger; this is 'One!'

Then what is another 'One'? 'Another one'?

This 'another' worked as the sesame *(Sim-Sim khul jaa!)* of *Aleebaba's* cave of forty thieves. As soon as I heard this term 'another' call me, I raised yet another finger, alongside the former one. In fact, all along in my perception I could not think that there might be some another 'one', as well. I was raising only one finger so far and trying to do the sum of that single 'One'. The singularity!

Now I had two fingers raised before me! I evoked my lovely mother for further help, "*Beebee*, help me." She came rushing. I showed him the two raised fingers and asked him, "*Beebee*, this is One, okay? And this is another One, okay? Now how to add both of them?"

"Join them together! Two, as simple as that! If that's what you call addition!", my mother spoke aloud, even as, excitedly.

"Oh, that is the answer! I know the answer; for at school, the students and the teacher were heard chanting the correct answer as 'Two'. Nonetheless, how this 'Two' had been arrived at? How this solution had been derived, I had not fathomed at school."

"One! Two!", my mother counted both the fingers in a breath, "This is One, this is yet another One; both joined together make Two: one, two!"

I then repeated the whole exercise myself to ensure that the mother was not making any mistake. When I finished counting one, two, it seemed as though the entire fortress of darkness and ignorance had crumbled with a bang before the eye of my mind! Big Bang! "That's it!", I shouted in exuberance and excitement. I had found the solution to the most intractable problem of the world: One plus One! Big Bang! This was like the *Eureka* of *Archimedes!*

Having attained to this unimaginable debut, the pioneering success in arithmetic, I felt as though

I had got the Master Key to all the problems of mathematics. As though the sesame to *Alee Baba's* cave of forty thieves had been procured. I tried my hands on other digits, like one plus two, two plus two etc. and was able to do them quite easily thenceforth. My heart swelled with pride, with self-esteem, with self-confidence, rather. Now there would be no humiliation for me at school from the very next day! I relished the thought.

Thereafter, the sums of arithmetic and mathematics became the game of my left hand, not only in my school, but throughout my life. There has been no looking back thereafter.

In the process, nonetheless, I realised that since my parents were absolute ciphers in arithmetic and mathematics, for that matter, and that they were perfect failures in their worldly pursuits, as well, exactly because of this lacuna; for in my conviction, the life is a very tough mathematics and solving the riddles of life is not the cup of tea of any Tom, Dick and Harry. One who is weak at mathematics is poor in life, too; this has been my experience based on empirical data.

Also, I realised that the most intractable issue of the world is to link one with another one! Figure-wise as well as figuratively!

XXX

32. Virtues May Land One In The Wilds Of Antagonism, Too.

Enter Protagonist

With the solving of 'one plus one' rigmarole as though the *mantra* of *'sesame'* had been discovered, as though *'Eureka'* had been pronounced, as though serendipity had resolved it: following the humiliation by the insensitive words of my father: 'Oh, now, you do not know even this? What an ill-luck!'

I entertained perpetual hatred for my parent for these insensitive words; but I feel, had he not uttered those hammering words to me, the locks of my treasure trove of self-wisdom, the *Bodhi*, would not have been opened. Neither my teachers explained to me what 'one plus one' signified, nor did my insensitive, nay, unmathematical, unmethodical father; it was me only, my humiliation *per se,* that summarily cracked the nut and the knot for me of 'one plus one', that is, two! As though the stroke of condemnation worked as the strike of a hammer on a cocoanut to crack it open!

And there was no looking back thereafter as I see! I became extraordinarily happy. I repeated my pleasure umpteen number of times to my mother and she shared my joy, too, boosting my morale in the process. She asked me to do other sums too and I did. It was so simple thereafter to do one plus two or one plus three or *vice versa*, that is, two plus one or three plus one. It had become a game now: game of left hand for me! I was now equipped with the *siddhi* to solve all the arithmetical problems.

When my father came home, my mother shared my extraordinary achievement with him, but he could hardly fathom the import of such nuances; my mother could. Father lacked that faculty of coming down to the level of a child's psyche. My mother knew well that the most intractable problem in the world was to solve 'one plus one' on one's own for the first time; if that gets cracked, there is no other problem left thereafter in the whole world!

The next day, when I reached school, I was a totally transformed persona; as though a metamorphosis had taken place from a caterpillar to a butterfly! I was no more a duffer, no more a clown of the class, no more a butt of joke for my classmates, my playmates. I was solving the questions with extraordinary alacrity as well as swiftness, promptness as well as exactitude. My teachers, who considered me a gone case till yesterday evening as far as mathematics was concerned, were stupefied to notice this miraculous transformation. Their favourite as well as beloved disciples, their brilliant students, were lagging behind most surprisingly and I was

running ahead of them by miles together, not by inches, almost like a hare vaulting ahead of the turtles! Miraculously, I had become a crown prince of the class as well as of entire school within no time. Until yesterday evening I was a clown, today abruptly I wore a crown! Strange are the workings of mother Nature, of Providence!

The companions and the teachers first thought, on first day, that it was a rare chance happening that I had done the sums; the next day too, they hoped alike, but when the feat kept on repeating unbrokenly and without breach, they started getting shocked: what had happened to this duffer, from where had come about this changeover about this proclaimed rascal? How had the buffoon that was *Kaaleedaas* till recently become a great scholar, having been humiliated at the hands of *Vidyottamaa* in the manner of my father? There ensued a buzz in the *Aadarsh Paathshaalaa*; there had happened a miracle in the school: a duffer, a *Kaaleedaas* had metamorphosed into *Vidyottamaa* or a great litterateur! I was revelling in my newfound *siddhi,* as well.

My classmate who had wrestled with me the other day on the way had now turned my friend, discovering that I was now a child prodigy and a rising sun; everybody bows to a rising sun! Incidentally, the same guy was in the habit of bringing some good-looking illustrated booklets from his home to the school and in the school, we used to read the stories both fictional and historical from those books. Those booklets or comics were also like *Aleebaba's* cave of treasure of forty thieves for us kids.

In those books only did we read about *Raama*'s story, the *Raamaayana*. And our story-teller teacher had already apprised us that *Raama* was a historical persona, and that, *Raamaayana* and *Mahaabhaarata* were historical chronicles of ancient India. Not only this, at our maternal uncle's home in *Nanihaal* too, our cousins – elder cousins, that is, the daughters of our maternal uncle – used to tell us daily at the time of going to bed the tales of *Raamaayana* sequentially and in a very interesting manner. The story of *Raama* itself is quite engrossing and our cousin's style of telling those tales rendered them exquisitely interesting. We children craved evening time for the purpose of listening to *Raama*'s stories by our cousins. Here at school, the same phenomenon was being repeated through these graphic books, the comics. Now we became doubly sure that the *Raama*'s story was true as well as historical.

Nonetheless, when we were reading the booklet – the comics – a curiosity crossed my mind: if *Raama* was actually born in *Ayodhyaa* and if there was an *Ayodhyaa* ever actually,

that should still be in existence on this earth and in India; there must be a spot where *Raama* would have been born. If he was really so great as to be the protagonist of an epic like *Raamaayana*! I put this question to my classmate who seemed to be the wisest amongst us all by that time so far as common sense was concerned. He replied that he did not know whether any *Ayodhyaa* was actually in existence, or where *Raama* was born. And the curiosity died or subsided there itself.

Nonetheless, the seed of curiosity had been shelved in the bosom of subconscious mind. Later on, after over two decades, when I entered the service arena and travelled throughout India, I was informed by one of my hosts at *Vaaraanasee* that a big issue was about to come up before the court for deciding. He also clarified that this was going to come after over half a century. I enquired him quizzically and he apprised me that it was *Raama*'s birthplace in *Ayodhyaa* that was under dispute since immediately after *Aazaadee*, the Independence, that is, the departure of Britishers and the handing over of power to the new regime of Indian politicians, dismantling the old guard of princes and *zamindaars* and the feudal set-up.

As soon as he disclosed this magical mystery to me, I was pleasantly stunned: it meant my query at my primary school that there must be a place where *Raama* would have been born if indeed there was a historical persona ever, was not off the mark. I wondered at the coincidence of this revelation and the eruption of my decades old curiosity at this point of time! Well, *Raama* was actually there. *Raama* had been relegated to dust with the onslaught of *Muslim* invaders who had raged the memorial of *Raama*, that is, the temple, to dust and erected thereon a mosque. Since times were against the followers and worshippers of *Raama*, they were helpless. But times keep on changing; none of the erstwhile kingdoms and *sultanates* are now in sight or existence, nor even the relatively recent princely states; with the demise of those autocrats, the followers of ancient culture have started reasserting themselves and have been trying to retrieve their forfeited glory.

This speaks volumes about the cycle of time: which has both vicious and virtuous aspects to it!

Anyways, I was now a prodigy both at school and at village. My school teachers conveyed this happy augury to my father, and my playmates were coming under my awe gradually as well as surprisingly. In the process, my chum, the story-teller boy was also overtaken by me; by that time he was considered more intelligent than I was. Now all of a sudden he found me in lead and naturally he started feeling jealous.

Nonetheless, he was confident that my wisdom was a chance happening and that soon I should lose steam and he would gain supremacy over me once again. This was the hope that kept him floating and not vitiating his friendship with me. However, he did not mince words in expressing his amazement at my sudden changeover from a duffer to a miraculous prodigy.

But the topper of the class – *Chiranjee*, or *Chiranjeev* – was not amused. He was an unchallenged champion of the class and school thus far. Suddenly, without an inkling, a duffer and dumb boy had metamorphosed into a prodigy overnight. *Chiranjee's* countenance underwent change and became furious. I could not fathom the reason of this change in *Chiranjee's* behaviour. I was simply intelligent for myself, I had not snatched away anything from *Chiranjee* or any other classmate; they had their own wisdom and intelligence intact with them; still their approach and attitude towards me had undergone drastic change. They loved me when I was a duffer since I posed no challenge to their prestige and position, myself being a duffer; however, now as I had become intelligent, I felt they no longer loved or liked me since I had become a challenge for them for retaining or preserving their prestige or position. Throughout my school days I kept on wondering why

Chiranjee hated me: because I was more brilliant than he was!

During exams, incidentally, I was fond of coloured question papers intuitively. I craved question papers. However, till 2nd grade, our teachers did not give us question papers when they took our exams. And we envied upper class students who got question papers – those multicoloured pamphlets! I longed for those.

In 3rd grade, when we got question papers for the first time, I got so much elated: I not only did the paper cent-percent correctly, but also, preserved the coloured question papers intact, without any folds or crease thereon, without their corners turned, i.e. dog-eared. I was so much infatuated with the question papers – I don't know why – that I preserved them for decades together unfolded and unmutilated. It was only later on when I realised that it was all foolishness, and that there was a question papers galore in the universe, and also, a problems galore all around throughout a man's lifetime, that I threw away the question papers of childhood or school days. The questionnaire of lifetime itself is so lengthy and cumbersome that there is no respite from them till the end of life!

Back to school, in the exam, I excelled and beat *Chiranjee*, what to speak of other friends. It was a riotous situation. Embarrassing for both teachers and students. How could a duffer beat a top student in competition! The saddening news reached the parents and relatives of *Chiranjee*; they lived in the neighbourhood of school only and had a clout in the town and on the school fraternity. They got immediately enraged: how could that be? How could *Chiranjee* be relegated to second place in the class or school? *Chiranjee* was invincible! *Chiranjee,* too, went to his parents gibbering and muttering all sorts of absurd things against school set-up, and also, against me – an innocent me.

I along with other children as usual followed *Chiranjee* to his shop innocently and unassumingly – his parents were traders, shop-keepers. There we heard his parents and uncles blasting against the school teachers that they had done grave injustice to their ward. Their grudge and apprehension was that the teachers had made a duffer the champion of the class, for the latter was the son of a teacher. I wondered; I was stupefied at the madness of those adults. What was my fault, I was wondering, if their ward had receded behind me? I had not snatched away his place. I was excelling in my position. Of my own virtues! Without malice towards anyone!

For the first time I realised that even to become virtuous or intelligent in school or elsewhere itself becomes a cause of antagonism towards one. The wilderness of the arena of literacy is so fierce! Although there was no risk of physical harm to me given my father himself being a teacher in the same town and having a clout amongst those traders as well, yet the mental botheration and the bewilderment lurked in my mind and it continued for years together until I left the school under the burden of circumstances. Might be to the relief of *Chiranjee* and his parents!

XXX

33. Grandpa's Tales At Our Khedaa

Enter Protagonist

In the entire narrative I am somehow omitting the mention of my family's habitat. In fact, our male members resided at a separate place other than that meant for female members. The female compounds were surrounded on all sides whereas the male habitats were by and large open expanses. In that sprawling space, as if figuratively, all the domestic cattle lived, too, as if to afford company to their male members. The cattle were like members of the family only: the cows, buffaloes, bullocks, calves etc. Stench of cow dung and cattle dung did permeate the atmosphere all the time; but it is also true, one who lives in the stench or odour constantly does not feel the bad smell, loses sense of smell.

Our *Khedaa,* that is, the male residence was on an elevated platform, almost two to three metres high as compared to the adjoining level of land where other residences were built. I could never fathom the mystery of this elevation of the *Khedaa*. To my mind, it represented the high status of the family in the village, just like that of war-lords as they *de facto* were.

On this *Khedaa*, which was quite wide, there were two buildings, one on each end of the platform. These were long rooms, each from one end to the other of the edge; almost twenty metres long each; mind metres, not feet! These halls were *kutcha,* of course, but built sturdily and seemed to be quite durable. The roofs were thatched and supported on wooden logs. These were the halls where the family had seen the golden days, the heydays of its pedigree during *British Raaj.* By the time we came to our senses, though, the grace had gone and penury had started setting in, revealing its fangs. Despondency had set in. The old guard had passed on and the new generation had taken over. All degraded version!

When I say *Khedaa*, I mean the residences of my grandfather and one more cousin of his. There were other such magnificent and high buildings all around for other elders of the family. The entire scene and scenario gave the impression of regal residences. The gates and doors of these buildings, though *kutcha*, were very high and spectacularly grandiose. And the inhabitants were considered to be very great, having a great clout in the area.

Anyway, with the departure of Britishers it seemed as though the grace and worth of the family had also departed! They exhibited themselves as conventionally as well as politically pleased expressing that the '*Aazadee*' had brought some abstract gains for everybody; nonetheless, somewhere in their hearts, contemplating about the changing circumstances and equations of power and wealth in the new dispensation, they had started feeling that the '*Aazaadee*' meant nothing but devastation of their wealthy set-ups and their authority. Also, usurpation of their privileges by the new breed of rulers, the lawyers, the stooges of Britishers. They were finding themselves entirely unequal to the rapidly changing challenges of coping with the fluid and wily circumstances of the country, rather, three and a half countries, of late: *Bhaarat, Paakistaan, Baangladesh* and, of course, *Jammoo & Kashmeer* as a half country.

In lieu of servants and helpers, as they used to employ by then, they had now started using their own hands and deploying their own physical labour for running the errands of their households. Earlier, during their heydays, it was entirely unimaginable a prospect! So far so that even a person like my grandfather had started putting in manual labour in household chores presently.

Nonetheless, I observed in my child's eye that my father was an exception still. He had no concern for agricultural or any other sort of household chores, nor did we children have a feeling that we had any agricultural holdings. All around us there used to be buzz about agricultural activities including in the house of our real elder uncle, but never in our personal household; and I wondered and felt a sense of deprivation at this situation. Also, I felt an inferiority complex: why my father didn't have any say in these interesting pursuits? But that was it! He was an *ad hoc* teacher in the town school and being myopic in senses he could never think that an *ad hoc* is an *ad hoc* and could be shunted out any time. Still, he harboured the notion that being the scion of landlords, of feudal set-up, his status would never change and that he would continue as an *ad hoc* in that school permanently. As though *ad hoc* meant 'permanent'!

Any type of sense of permanency engenders arrogance and hallucination. My father seemed to be harbouring the notions of permanency in respect of both life and employment, with the result that he was very rude and cruel towards one and all. He could never think that his stay on the planet was *ad hoc*, too, and that his job in the school was apparently *ad hoc*. I sometimes wondered how a person could be so blind to Creation's realities as my father was!

But, I observed that most of the persons acknowledged that my father was a deranged and insane personality; I had overheard many of his near and dear friends commenting like this to his back and deriding him and his behaviour; albeit they flattered him to his face whenever the opportunity occasioned itself. I rued their hypocrisy and their reality. The astute guys never call a spade a spade; they flatter a duffer to no end, for therein lies their benediction!

In such circumstances we were living in that half room, shared with our elder aunt. We, that is, my father didn't have any milch cattle of his own. The families were nuclear families, no joint families by the time I gained senses. Everybody had to fend for oneself and nobody came to anybody's rescue howsoever closely related one might be. In the process, the kids like our father's suffered tremendously as well as psychologically; they developed complexes. Unbeknown to father! But our insolent father was

unconcerned; he was more concerned about his own personal upkeep and career – non-existent one!

Our grandfather stayed and had his food arrangement with our elder uncle; my father could never afford to feed him for he himself was always short of foodgrains: for himself and his issues. And I rued this situation thinking that our grandfather was not our grandfather in the real sense in which one's blood relations should have food from the same kitchen. How could we say that he was our grandfather because he was never having food with us, from our homestead. Still, blood relation was there if only notionally, and our grandfather showed the same amount of affection towards us as he had for the issues of our elder uncle's – *taujee's*.

In the evenings, after finishing his daily chores related to agricultural fields and the cattle and his chats at the bonfire with his elder brother -- cousin -- and other prominent personages of the village, when he returned to his cot towards our end of the *Khedaa* – on one end resided his cousin and on the other resided our grandfather – he told us the stories. All other old men of the family had already passed away. We children, one or two I think, surrounded our grandfather and entreated him to tell us tales or biographies of great men. Those were the days when TV was not even conceptualised yet and even radio was in its rudimentary stage. It was only the instrumentality of the voice as well as the vocal cord of grandfathers and grandmothers that children drew entertainment and imbibed the elements of culture including instructions about norms of living through stories and classic epics.

My grandfather being an English educated rarity of a persona of the area, we had an added advantage of his reservoir of bookish knowledge. He told us one or two stories in minute details stretching it to their extreme extents, to our amusement and pleasure, and in the process, we kids would doze off and ultimately sleep. That was the ultimate aim of those tales to be told by our grandfather; listening to stories from the mouth of our grandfather we slept cozily, and we, too, requested our grandfather exactly with that aim only in mind. Moreover, through those stories of worldly knowledge the horizon of our minds was getting enlarged, to our pleasure and amazement. We wished that the sphere of stories and knowledge were endless and infinite.

In the process, I suppose, the grandpa had narrated to us verbally the stories of Gulliver's Travels and other world classics, like, Arabian Nights in his own tongue, to suit the taste and tongue of us children.

Finally, he was out of stock and started taking excuses, to our dismay. After all, how long can one fabricate tales or stories?

Nevertheless, we still miss those sessions of grandfather's stories! We had missed the sessions of storytelling by our teacher in *Aadarsh Paathshaalaa* at town school! Also, we had missed the evening time stories of *Raamaayana* told once upon a time by our maternal cousin, and we miss them even today! May God all those contributors to our mental and psychic horizon through stories live eternally in the bliss and blessings of God!

XXX

Table of Contents

34. My Supposed Lineage

Enter Protagonist

The frame of pictures or the pictures inside the frame keep on changing incessantly: not only the pictures, but also, the human beings that keep company with us – friends or foes; the cattle and other creatures – that we tame; the relations and kinsmen – that we adopt; the institutions and organisations – that we feel associated with; and our possessions – both material and mental; all undergo change at an unnoticeable pace, yet incessantly, unceasingly. Nevertheless, the landscape and the land themselves keep on changing their countenance: they never remain the same against the common perception that the land is inert thereby remaining as such for ever; that's not true. It also keeps on changing its scenes and scenarios, and its countenance.

From my childhood till date I have observed – and it needs no proof: seeing is believing – that the scene of my village and my family has been transforming constantly, and without the process *per se* coming into notice. That is the mystery and beauty of Nature's working; it does not come to notice when it's being done. It's only after a gap in time that our senses observe that there is a change that has taken place. Change *per se* – particularly, the Natural change – is such an imperceptible process that nobody can perceive it happening. That's Creator's beauty and testimony to His insuperability!

In my childhood, I observed all around in my family's household magnificent and high-ceilinged buildings, sprawling and vast fields, huge-sized trees with stems admeasuring in metres, cattle in large numbers – both milch and plough, that is, agriculture-worthy, that is, bullocks; also bulls – to impregnate the milch cattle like cows and buffaloes. The poor folks, that is, servant class which in time came to be known as lower caste and, of late, '*Dalits*' were not supposed to rear cows or buffaloes; they made do with such small-sized cattle as goats, sheep and pigs, which they not only

reared for milch, but also, for meat that was their staple food. Cereals were the prerogative of stronger class and the servants were left to the choice of meat. That is how lower strata of society was forced to become non-vegetarian: due to intransigence and self-centredness of upper echelons of society, the who's who of Indian culture. The buildings there were all *kutcha*, why, I don't know; may be due to brick-kilns not being in vogue those days. However, the walls of the houses were one and a half metre in thickness invariably. Today, when I observe the thickness of walls in 4 inches, I am astounded how much the man has changed, from one and half metres to merely four inches. That diminution in size of walls is reflected not only in their habitats, but also, as though in the size of their hearts! At that time, people were broad-hearted, broad-minded like their thick walls, unlike these days of thin partitions!

Moreover, they had a great clout in the area; they were supposed to be a very great family in the area. They might have had a banyan tree some time back, that's why they were still called *'Barhwaley'* which literally implies 'Big people' or 'those owning a Banyan tree'. *Barh* or *Bad* is double meaning word that means both 'big' and 'banyan tree'. Their relations were, as well, very wealthy and influential people: all as well as everywhere, without exception!

They were all landlords – *zamindaars*. They possessed large land-holdings. And I wondered in my child-like curiosity how all of them might have come to own such large tracts of lands in such a fertile area, that is, the basin of *Gangaa* and *Yamunaa*. That is considered to be the most fertile portion of the soil in India. Also, the same was the epicentre of all the battles and political tussles all through the history. To grab the land and property in this part of the country would take extraordinary power and clout. And that my ancestors were settled in this part, was a proof itself, a sort of truism, that they would have been sort of war-lords, invincible and extremely influential ones.

To satiate my curiosity, I put up this question to my grandfather one day at our story session. An additional cause of my wonderment was that whereas all those wealthy as well as insolent people were enjoying themselves in all sorts of comforts of food and habitat, there were others – and in umpteen numbers and majority – who didn't have even two morsels of food to eat a day, nor a roof of proper type over their heads. They were living in pathetic conditions and were seen clad in rags. Also, being tortured and humiliated by these influential people not infrequently, on this or that flimsy pretexts. Of course, those wretched lots were obliged to make

themselves employed under these wealthy farmers and got the latter's second-hand clothes for wearing condescendingly from their insolent masters. This situation no doubt used to perturb me a lot and did gnaw at my conscience consistently. How can human beings and society be so unjust? That too, towards their own clan, or species!

Also, I did notice that the names of most of the family members in our larger family were having prefixes of '*Sheo*' which, later on, I came to realise denoted '*Shiv*'. Definitely, my ancestors or those who were extant at that time were not devotees of lord *Shiva* as was obvious from the fact that they were *Aarya Samaajees* and did not pursue idolatry by and large with a few exceptions, particularly, on the part of ladies who adored *Chaamarh*. How they had come to be fond of using this '*Sheo*' prefix was a great mystery for me, sort of intrigue for me. Many of our aunts were *Sheodaan, Sheoraanee* etc, whereas many of our uncles were *Sheoraaj* and *Shoeveer et al*. There must be certainly some solid ground for this fascination for the prefix '*Sheo*'; I put this puzzle to my grandfather at the time of our evening story-telling session one day.

In fact, the poser put up to my grandfather was somewhat differently framed, not a direct one. Why I chose my grandfather only for solving this conundrum is because in my perception – and in the perception of multitudes of village folk and family members – he was the most sensible as well as the only knowledgeable person available within our wherewithal. And I was dead sure that my grandfather would be knowing the answer to this obvious puzzle.

I asked my grandfather when he was going to start some other tale for us kids. I asked, "*Baabaa*, from where have we come? Were we always living at this village? Or have we come from somewhere else? Since we are supposed to be royals – having a pedigree related to some regality -- as is obvious by circumstances, to whom actually is our ancestry related: to *Raama*, to *Krishna* or to whom in immediate historical annals?...."

Baabaajee paused for a while. He did not intend to sweep me away by simply saying he did not know. He said, "We seem to be related to *Maraathaas*, to *Shivaajee* in the recent annals of history!"

"But our elder *Baabaajee* tells us that we came from *Gujaraat* originally?"

"Our traditions, conventions and habits match with those of *Gujaraatees*, and that is true what elder brother has told you, for we hail from the lineage of lord *Krishna* of *Mahaabhaarata* repute. Nonetheless, I am telling you about the recent linkages."

He further added that in the militia of *Shivaajee*, there were *Jaadhavs*, that is, *Yaduvanshee kshatriyas,* that is *Jaadons*, alongside the *Maraathaas* as is well known from the history. *Shivaajee*'s mother – *Jeejaabaai* – was a *Yaduvanshee* lady and was very brave-hearted. In the due course, when other castes started using this appellation '*Yaadav*' for them, we changed our surname to '*Jaadon*' to differentiate ourselves from them. Still many an ignoramus does not believe this and they consider *Jaadon* and *Yaadav* as one and the same caste. This is the complexity associated with the evolution of castes. Though there is nothing wrong with the *Yaadavs* but they are not the same as us so far as lineage goes. We have, therefore, dropped this surname, of late, and have started using '*Singh*' or '*Raanaa*' for our clan. *Raanaa* implies one who fights battles – *Ran.* We also have a linkage with *Mahaaraana* as did *Shivaajee*, too.

I was so glad to come to know of this revelation: I was linked to *Shivaajee!* That's why in every talk in our family there used to be so much praise and regard for '*Shivaajee Mahaaraaj*' or '*Shivaajee Raaje*'!

XXX

35. *Legal Luminaries vs Technical Honchos*

Enter Grandfather

"How come our ancestors were so powerful?", asked my grandson when we were sitting together telling child stories.

I however availed this opportunity to apprise the young lads and lasses of the family annals.

"All our relations are influential and powerful, you see!", I clarified the obvious fact.

"Yes! And that is a matter of great puzzle."

"No puzzle! Actually, in our immediate ancestry, there were four brothers, begotten to a father who was warlord in the *Maraathaa* militia or you may even call it army. His appellation was '*Raajaa*', the king. *Raajaa Lakshman Singh*. King in fact does not necessarily connote the sovereign in Indian context; it rather implied a warlord or a vassal to the sovereign.

"You would observe also that none of our principalities were under *Muslim* lords, that is, *nawaabs* or princes, nor under *Hindoo* princely states; we were governed directly by *British Raaj*. I am talking of the time at *Aazaadee* and before that."

"This, in turn, also implies that our ancestors and relatives were all loyal to *British Raaj*!", interjected my grandson.

"That is obvious! They were loyal to Britishers. The obliging factor might be that they wielded huge powers and possessed humongous amounts of property both landed and monetary."

"Another reason might be that with a view to countering the *Muslim* authoritarians, *Muslim* tyrants, to be precise, they might have sided with Britishers who were more just, chaste and law-abiding, whereas under *Muslim* or even *Hindoo* princes there was no rule of law; they were law unto themselves," added my grandson.

"That's true! History has never been an issue worth bothering about or to be written about, especially in India. The Indian rulers never minded their victories or defeats, nor did they keep chronicles of their victories for posterity. Exact chain of events thus is not available so as to prove it empirically." I explained.

"Listen then! We have connection with *Gadh Raanaa* which implies connection with *Raanaas* of *Mewaar*. We have connections with *Gujaraat*; our conventions match with those of *Gujaraatees*. Our earlier most ancestor was *Shri Krishna* who was a *kshatriya* scion; though himself not a king but was considered to be a king of kings, a divinity. Such was his awe and clout! Our connection is with *Shivaajee Mahaaraaj* in whose army our ancestors were commanders, possibly, given our stature even today. Besides, one renowned princely state and prince of our caste was *Chhatrasaal Mahaaraaj* whose father was the famous king *Champat Rai*, warlord in the *Aurangzeb*'s army. He had helped *Aurangzeb* in the struggle for throne against the benevolent prince *Daaraa Sikoh;* and it was a grave mistake on his part, irrespective of the fact that *Chhatrasaal* was our ancestor!

"Some glare of their grandeur has been rubbed onto our stature!", I exclaimed laughingly.

"All renowned and venerable names of India's medieval history!", my grandson interjected.

"In fact everybody has such gifted ancestry to recall, whoever is alive today! Because those not related to powerful ancestry were all destroyed in the mayhem of history or they starved under the wheels of tyranny of feudalism and barbarism."

"*Baabaajee*, even at present, you have such powerful and influential persons as your connections!"

"That's because I was studying at *Aagaraa* and *Khurjaa* and they all are my classmates, who have attained to higher positions in Govt and administration. Actually, the number of students and classmates in those days was very few, that's why they maintained contacts among themselves lifelong, unlike these days when you do not know who your classmates are, for they are now

in hundreds; whom to recollect, whom to forget?

"Nonetheless, feudal lords as they are or were, they were rich and had all the vices of feudal lordships: they were insolent, cruel, arrogant, irritable, intemperate, dissipated etc. Liquor was their main drink and addiction."

"But you do not drink liquor, *Baabaajee*! Despite having company with Britishers and all the royals in your school?"

"It's not true. I can drink liquor, but I am not addicted. Liquor is a very good appetizer; if taken in small measures and along with nutritious diet it is a healthy drink. The Europeans take heavy diet with drinks, that's why they do not lose their head even after drinking heavily. On the contrary, our people are addicts; they do not eat nutritious foods, nor can they afford, nor do they have knowledge of what is nutritious and what not. They simply drink and lose their brains and fall in drainages, mad, half-conscious and senseless. Already they are *sans* any brains!"

"That is a news for me! I thought you were a teetotaller, for I have never seen you drink in my life," uttered my grandson visibly startled.

"That's true; I have not drunk for last many decades."

"And your cousins drink to their madness and use foul language against whoever comes in front of them!"

"That's a matter of grave concern."

"Did you never sound them in this regard?"

"Who cares? Even your father does not bother. He is my son!"

To this despondent and helpless remark of mine, my grandson smiled bemusingly.

"Not only this, many of our relatives are plunderers, waylayers: they waylay the poor travellers. They sit at the bridges of brooks in the evening and plunder and loot the travellers and commuters passing thereby. Sometimes they even murder them if the wayfarers resist. They even rape the females if they get to have the chance. Such demoniac beasts!

"Some of our relatives are marauders, they can kill anybody with impunity. And some of the relatives of our relatives or their connections are with the dacoits; I can cite you many instances."

"You are right *Baabaajee*. In our *Nanihaal*, a dacoity is reported to have taken place in the nearby hamlet long back when I was not even born. The victims were a family of two wealthy brothers. A dacoit known to our *Naanaajee*'s family had executed that dacoity there and killed the rich man – the father – sparing, of course, the sons, because their mother was reported to have taken her sons under her cover and pleaded with the devil to spare the sons. The devil was reported to have shouted roaringly, "My name is so and so, I have killed so and so, dare anybody challenge me?" and the gory night had shuddered with deadly dread. My mother had narrated this tale to me many a time. I was not born yet, when the dacoity took place. However, in the tone of my mother while narrating this gory episode and in enacting the threat of the bandit, there was a sense of latent perverse pride; and I always wondered why my mother always delivered those gory dialogues without any pathos towards the victim; rather, she seemed to be siding with the murderer. The mystery, however, got unfolded decades later when after serving his sentence for ten or fifteen years, the bandit came out of jail as an aged bodied bulky person and I incidentally sighted him sauntering around in our *nanihaal* and our maternal household beckoning him respectfully to their dwellings. However, he did not oblige and had simply departed. My *naanaa* and *naanee* disclosed to me after he had left that the same was the person who killed the father of *Yashpaal*.", clarified my grandson.

"Yeah, there are myriads of gory tales to tell. The human society is quite vulnerable and unstable in that respect. All our sense of security is based on the ill-conceived notion of human goodness and the efficacy of law and order machinery, whereas in reality both the factors are palpably absent. What power protects us at night and during the day on the way is a great mystery!

"They had very splendid buildings as their houses in their heydays but gradually their splendour is declining, the glow is dimming. They are becoming paupers. For they did not have the acumen to earn the livelihood in the absence of gratuitous *zamindaaree* proceeds which had been snatched away under the guise of *Aazaadee* by the new political class. This is not that only some of them are getting impoverished, all are, including us. Our buildings and habitats are also crumbling day by day and one by one. In lieu thereof, people are raising what may pass for slums or *jhuggee-jhonpadees* as they call it in urban centres."

"If our ancestors by chance happen to resurrect themselves and come to visit their erstwhile habitats and households, they would be stunned!", remarked my grandson.

"Why only ancestors, even those alive at present and not been to this place express shock at the decline," I added, "The other day recently when my niece, the daughter of my elder brother – *Netaajee* – happened to visit this village, she could not recognise her relatives and

the buildings; she remarked to the person accompanying her and searching for the habitats of her relatives that these could never be the houses of her ancestors!"

"Let us peep into the chain of events that led to this situation. *Mahaaraaj Chhatrasaal* was an associate of *Shivaajee* and a great admirer of his. And our ancestors were related to this king, in the process getting the appellation of king for our great grandfather. These large tracts of land in this *Gangetic* basin might have been allotted by *Mahaaraajaa Chhatrasaal* to him. Or maybe, during the fight with proverbial *Ahmed Shaah Abdaalee*, whereas the *Maraathaas* were vanquished by that fiend of an invader, however, later on the latter had reached up to *Delhi* and had sway over the entire north India. Being in the army as commanders, our ancestors might have dislodged the erstwhile landowners or might have put them to sword and usurped the lands. They contend, *Muslims* ruled the country; if that's true, how come not they but our ancestors and most other *Hindoos* control almost the entire stock of arable land in northern India?

"Like everything changes, the cycle of status of man also changes. Neither *Shivaajee Mahaaraaj* is there, nor his heirs, presently; they were all dislodged by their wily courtiers and the latter started ruling the roost. Neither *Chhatrasaal Mahaaraaj* is there now, nor his heirs to be seen anywhere anymore; instead, we as commoners are here discoursing the turn of events in the light of new regime in place. *Muslims* decimated *Hindoo* kings; and Britishers decimated *Muslim* kings, even *Hindoo* princes. Now, these lawyers have decimated both princes and Britishers and they are now ruling the roost and calling themselves '*Netaas*'."

"Mere deceptive change of designation, *Baabaajee!* Earlier, they were called *Samraat, Mahaaraaj, Sultaan, Baadshaah, Nawaab, Raajaa* etc; now they have changed that designation to '*Netaa*' merely to hoodwink the gullible subjects. Their entitlements are the same as were those of erstwhile rulers and autocrats. Rather much higher! Their activities are equally mean and sordid. What we call mafia these days was actually called ruler in earlier epochs, whatever appellation they might have adopted notwithstanding. Mafia is called one who has not got power to govern others, otherwise whoever has got the power to govern or rule is nothing but mafiosi only, but can't be called as such, or else, the caller might be put to sword, or to gun, these days.", summed up my grandson and I was stupefied to hear that rulers were mafiosi only who could not be called

as such and were, therefore, called by disparate designations, to instil a sense of fear and terror in the hearts of subjects.

"Kings as well as autocratic rulers did evolve eventually through this process only, you are true! A bandit would form a band of some dacoits and they would keep on terrorising others and enlarging their counts and strength; and when they would become invincible, they would thrust themselves upon the vanquished people, declaring themselves as kings or *baadshahs* or *raajaas*. That's true!" I clarified.

"However much ennobled or aggrandized we may feel to think that we are the heirs to such great lineage, the reality is that we are presently mere commoners whom nobody minds and everybody considers as weaklings. However, the present dispensation must take cue from this narrative in that like all others have vanished and have been overtaken by some other system or dispensation, this dispensation of lawyers will also come to an end one day and will be overtaken by some other form or system, possibly by technocrats or technical honchos." I concluded.

XXX

The End

English Books by *'Videh'*

Hypocrisy & Reality (fiction series: 9 books)

'Hypocrisy & Reality' is a fiction series comprising multiple books – novels. The fiction is aimed at depicting the hypocrisy of human society in every respect, be it the upbringing and treatment of babies, toddlers, children, adolescents, youths, or be it the treatment meted out to adults, aged ones, those who are closely related with oneself, with one's blood; not to speak of those called strangers or outsiders. Barring a rarity, nobody cares two hoots for the sentiments or security and safety of other living creatures on this sole planet nurturing 'living' beings!

Book 1: Beyond the Pale (fiction)

'Beyond the Pale' of Time & Space is the first volume of the long fiction series 'Hypocrisy & Reality' and as the name suggests, it deals with the timespan in the life of the protagonist when one had not even had a tryst with the concepts of Time and Space, nor did they make any difference in one's life if those ubiquitous phenomena were not taken cognizance of. Those were the years before the realm of schooling, the arena of perfect unconcern for the written letters, words, or numbers.

Book 2: Wilderness of Literacy (fiction)

'Wilderness of Literacy' is the second volume in the long fiction series 'Hypocrisy & Reality' and, as the name suggests, it takes the protagonist in the arena of letters, words, and numbers: the realm of what we call the 'literacy'. The experience of a child while treading this seemingly dreaded as well as untrodden landscape is nothing short of venturing into a wilderness; of course, led and mentored first by one's parents and thereafter invariably by their preceptors -- the masters -- all of whom have a tremendous amount of impact on the future human being that emerges from their inputs given and endeavours made towards making a man, the humanity.

Book 3: Advent of Time (fiction)

'Advent of Time' is the third volume in the long fiction series entitled 'Hypocrisy & Reality' and covers the schooling period when the protagonist discovered the phenomenon of Time, and also, figuratively he felt that it was then his time, even as, he mysteriously discovered his latent potential and wisdom catapulting himself into the uppermost orbits of glory, fame and all round applause from his classmates, masters as well as teachers. To his own amazement as well as bewilderment! Nevertheless, this providential blessing was not without its blemishes in the shape of rancour and envy of fellow classmates and their patrons towards him. Even as, Nature never allows anybody pleasure and praise without at the same time associating with them the equivalent amount of pain and back-biting!

Book 4: Devoid of Shelter (fiction)

'Devoid of Shelter', the fourth volume in the long fiction series 'Hypocrisy & Reality' furthers the journey of the protagonist into the world where he discovered to his dismay that he had no place on the globe which he could call as his home; he had no place of his own where he could take shelter during the day, and during the night. He somehow made do with seeking shelter with the relatives – maternal chiefly; not as a transitory phenomenon, but for good, until he himself took command of his life, snatching himself away from the indolent lifestyle of his parents. He also discovered during the refuge that however meritorious one might be, without the good base of ancestry, one was not considered as such.

Book 5: Price of Refuge (fiction)

'Price of Refuge', the fifth volume in the fiction series 'Hypocrisy & Reality' furthers the journey of the protagonist into the world when he returned to his paternal relatives and found to his dismay that his father was absolutely incapable of arranging a dwelling of his own. Also, he found himself to be a mute subject to child abuse at the hands of none other than supposedly an elder cousin of his, the son of his so-called benefactors who provided refuge in their vacant house. That was the price paid by the child for the indolence and handicaps of an unworthy father for seeking shelter under the tutelage of so-called relatives. No refuge seemingly looking innocuous goes without some price to be paid either by self, spouse or one's children.

Book 6: Hatred towards Love (fiction)

'Hatred towards Love', the sixth volume in the fiction series 'Hypocrisy & Reality' furthers the journey of the protagonist into the world where to his amusement he found himself catapulted into the realm of a celebrity or at least a child prodigy as far as the small rural catchment area was concerned. By virtue of his giftedness in the realm of studies and his bewitching countenance, the classmates, especially, the lasses of her age could not help restraining themselves from loving him; and they did it overtly, without caring for the opinions and feelings of other class-fellows. Albeit the protagonist himself wallowed in the faulty ideology that having any truck with fair sex was anathema and a great sin which could not be washed away in later life.

Book 7: Towards the Yoga (fiction)

'Towards the Yoga', the seventh volume in the fiction series 'Hypocrisy & Reality' dwells on the period in the journey of life of the protagonist when he was at the pinnacle of his bodily prowess and psychic acuity, thanks to his habit of pursuing *Yogaasans* regularly as well as religiously. As though something divine was associated with the pursuit of *Yogaasans*, his father luckily could get an *ad hoc* teacher's job in the town school too; however, that was not to be sustained throughout for at the fag-end of the academic session, his father fell out with the Principal of school and was expelled. *Yoga,* nevertheless, gave the protagonist a hue that was unparalleled, and which materialised into the worldly as well as societal fame for him.

Book 8: On the Descent (fiction)

'On the Descent', the eighth volume in the fiction series 'Hypocrisy & Reality' takes the protagonist over the hump. He was then a ward of such a guardian who did not have any wherewithal to run his household, yet had no qualms about begetting more issues, more and more at that. Agriculture, of course, he had as an inheritance but he was by nature averse to anything even distantly associated with agriculture or Nature, for that matter. Any industrious as well as expedient agriculturalist would have eked out one's livelihood quite easily from the fifteen *beeghaa*s of arable land his father had inherited from his resourceful, brave as well as powerful ancestors, but not he.

Book 9: In the Exile (fiction)

'In the Exile', the ninth volume in the fiction series 'Hypocrisy & Reality' furthers the journey of the protagonist into the world where post his dramatic jump into the orbit of fame in the wake of his High School result, he found himself entirely in a barren land where he could see no ray of hope from his father, even as, the latter was totally incapable of arranging the means to further the studies for his exceptionally gifted son. For the first time, the protagonist realised that his father was incapable of meeting his requirements for pursuing further studies. He was already suffering emotionally having been separated from his mother for the first time! This was for him like an exile, that too, very uncomfortable!

Bewailing Muse (poetry)

Be it the sage *Valmeeki* or be it the modern poet *Sumitraa Nandan Pant*, both have held that poetry has its founts in heart and is the outcome of extreme sorrow, misery or pangs of separation. Poetry cannot be created; it gets engendered out of compulsion. From the heart! Heart's language is poetry or musing! I have offered to christen them as Muse: 'Bewailing Muse'; the first musings out of wailings! Nevertheless, I am tempted not to treat them as children's literature for I sense some substantial element, too, in them. The period of the composition of these poems is from 1972 to 1976; and I feel that my wailings have not fallen on deaf ears, so to say, given my present circumstances of life which are totally opposite to the then prevailing ones!

Chambellion (drama: comedietta)

In the genre of Drama (Comedietta), here is the playlet *'Chambellion'* that exposes the bizarre reality of the political developments post transfer of reins from the whites to the yellow people in the guise of 'Democracy' and 'Independence'; whereas actually the latter have been pursuing their dynastic agenda and propagating their own family fiefdoms that have flourished like weeds in multitudes in the void created by annihilation of Princely states and Landlords. Allegorically, it may be compared with the weed flourishing in an agricultural field which has remained unsown after harvest of the previous crop. For the subjects, verily, there is no Freedom whatsoever, in literal sense.

Brainy Beasts (short stories)

This is an anthology of short stories, included wherein are four short stories or farces, so to say, that is, anecdotes including the 'In An Illegible Script', which is the English version of the author's *Hindee* short story '*Anpadh Lipi Mein...* (अनपढ़ लिपि में)' that was first published in now extinct though the then prestigious *Hindee* magazine the '*Kaadambinee'* way back in July, 1992, with quite an applause and accolades from the sides of kind readers! Other stories or anecdotes are also those published in other places, i.e. journals of variegated hues. Nothing uttered in these works is meaningless; this conviction is at work behind the inspiration to publish them in book form for kind readers.

Search for Life (translation of 'Hatyaaree Sadee Mein Jeevan Kee Khoj' (हत्यारी सदी में जीवन की खोज))
English Translation by *'Videh' Arvind Kumar* of *Hindee* poetry book *'Hatyaaree Sadee Mein Jeevan Kee Khoj' (हत्यारी सदी में जीवन की खोज)* by renowned young poet *'Nirvikaar' Mukesh Kumar*. This book has earned *'Nirvikaar'* the award of *'Jai Shankar Prasaad Puraskaar'* of Rs. One Lac from the *'Rajya Karmchaaree Saahitya Sansthaan, Uttar Pradesh'*. On the *Hindee* book *'Hatyaaree Sadee Mein Jeevan Kee Khoj,'* critiques by renowned personalities -- both young and old -- like *Ashwaghosh, Prempaal Sharmaa, Rajeev Saxena, Dr Anoop Singh, Dr Devkee Nandan Sharmaa, Manoj Kumaar Jhaa, Gautam Rajarshi*, etc have been published in various journals and magazines. The renowned critic Dr *Om Nishchal* has included this anthology in the select category for *'Kavya Paridrishya'* of 2017 amongst the famous poetry books.

Reality of Invisible (translation of 'Adrishya Kaa Yathaarth' (अदृश्य का यथार्थ))
English translation by *'Videh' Arvind Kumar* of the *Hindee* poetry book *'Adrishya Kaa Yathaarth' (अदृश्य का यथार्थ)* by renowned poet *'Ashwaghosh' Om Prakaash Sharmaa. 'Ashwaghosh'* -- a well-known moniker of *Hindee*

Procreation, the Adorable (English summary of Shiv Puraan)
The *Shiva-ling* has ever been a matter of

world! A litterateur of impeccable renown! Praised by multitudes -- both in literary and plebeian spheres! He has been composing prolifically -- having published over two dozen books spanning all the genre! The thesis, the short stories, the short epics, the anthologies, the new genre songs, the *ghazals*, the poetry for children *et al.* Covering all age groups! He has been honoured with many awards in literary and academic fields by prestigious institutions.

Nagasaki: Bomb & Aftermath (commentary on the first novel of Nobel Laureate, Kazuo Ishiguro) (Displayed on Oxford bookstore)
This is a work of literary study into the first novel 'The Pale View of Hills' by 2017 Literature Nobel Laureate, Kazuo Ishiguro, who has narrated in a mesmerising style of story telling the tale of Japanese society undergoing change in the aftermath of dropping of atomic bomb. The Americans not only vanquished and occupied the Japanese military and land by dropping the most lethal weapon never before heard of – the atomic bomb – on two of the Japanese cities, one of which was Nagasaki which witnessed this technological devastation on 8th of August, 1945, but also, occupied the minds and hearts of Japanese youth, both men and women. The youth of Japan started decrying everything old and conventional including their erstwhile education system and the ideologies of patriotism and nationalism.

amazement and mystery for mankind. That something obscure is there behind the adoration of such a carnal symbol as *ling* irrespective of the same being that of a deity called *Shiva* has ever been lingering in my mind. Why should a large majority of population in this land – from north to south -- worship the genitals so openly, so brazenly? So reverently! *Shiva* is supposed to be a mythological persona, in existence too long back in time, who might have been the pioneer in realizing the spectacular qualities of *ling* and *yoni,* specifically, those of converting the *sthaavar* (the insensate) into *jangam* (the sensate) and those of creating the *satva-lok,* (conscious beings).

Self-Styled Sovereign, the Judiciary

(Dramatic deliberation on the state of judiciary)

This is in fact an academic deliberation on the functioning and reality of the judicial system prevalent in India post what they euphemistically call the 'Independence' or, literally, the *'Aazaadee'.* Whose Independence was it anyway? For whom? Except for the ruling class? The lawyers first, and then the hooligans of *Chambal.* Nonetheless, the judiciary of the free country turned out to be one step further than its new crop of leaders; they usurped the entire authority from the latter in subtle moves one after the other. In olden epochs, the autocratic *Sultaans* or *Baadshaahs* dispensed justice purely depending upon their whims and fancies, which were incidental to the moods and tantrums of the Sovereign. Historically as well, the Real Sovereign was the one who dispensed justice. The Judiciary in Indian Republic soon realised this and acted.

XXX

'विदेह' रचित हिंदी ग्रंथ

अनपढ़ लिपि (कहानी-संग्रह)

'विदेह' अरविन्द कुमार की आठ हिंदी कहानियों का संकलन! संकलन की पहली कहानी 'अनपढ लिपि में ...' जुलाई, 1992 में प्रतिष्ठित हिंदी पत्रिका 'कादंबिनी' में छपी थी। 'सिग्नेचर' भी स्वच्छता के प्रति सरकारी महकमे की विद्रूपात्मक मनोदशा का कड़वा चित्रण है। 'ताकि आप अपने पक्ष में रहें!' नये प्रकार के कर्मचारियों की मानसिकता को इंगित करती है। 'फिर फिर वही लोग' भेड़-बकरियों की तरह दुरुपयोग किये जा रहे जन-समुदाय के विषय में कहानी है। 'अपार्थाइड' : वस्तुतः तो, शक्तिशाली और निर्बल का भेद ही असली रंग-भेद है। नया वेद' 'आज़ादी' नाम से वही पारम्परिक पद्धति चतुराई-पूर्वक 'नया संविधान' के नाम से चलाये जाने की पोल-पट्टी खोलती है। 'पहली कमाई' कहानी का आख्यान कल्पना से भी अधिक विस्मयकारी है! 'भगवान को पैसा' समाज और सरकार दोनों ही की धन के प्रति जो दृष्टि है, उस पर तीखा व्यंग्य है।

पाषाण-युग (कहानी-संग्रह)

'विदेह' अरविन्द कुमार की सात हिंदी कहानियों का संकलन! संकलन की पहली कहानी 'ब्लॉक का पेड़' आज के समाज में क्षीण होते हुए आपसी सौहार्द्र, एवं अजनबियों के प्रति बढ़ते अकारण वैमनस्य, को बिंबित करती हुई सच्चाई है। 'मेरी ज्ञाति' भारत में जातियों के हास्यास्पद 'प्रहसन' – फ़ार्स (farce) -- को चित्रित करके इसकी विद्रूपता को व्यंजित करती है। 'हिंदू-मुसलमान' साम्प्रदायिकता के प्रश्न को व्यक्तियों – दो घनिष्ट मित्रों -- के स्तर पर परीक्षण करके देखती है। 'मुर्गबाज' समय की नब्ज पर हाथ रखने की कोशिश है। 'मंदिरों, मस्जिदों, गुरुद्वारों, गिरजाघरों में ...' साम्प्रदायिक कट्टरता की निरर्थकता को व्यंजित करने के लिए है, जो मृत्यु के पर्दे के पीछे कितनी हास्यास्पद बन जाती है! 'ऐ अधर्मी!' आदमी की नश्ल को बदलने की नाहक कोशिश कही जा सकती है। 'राक्षस' इस नये शासन-प्रशासन में व्याप्त

भ्रष्टाचार पर एक व्यंग्यात्मक टिप्पणी है, और बताती है कि राक्षस कोई कपोल-कल्पना नहीं है, बल्कि आज भी एक वास्तविकता है।

निसर्ग (कहानी-संग्रह)

'विदेह' अरविन्द कुमार की सात हिंदी कहानियों का संकलन! संकलन की पहली कहानी 'मुलाक़ात एक बड़े लेखक से' एक बड़े लेखक और एक आम आदमी के जीवन के साम्य और अंतर दोनों को ही उजागर करती है। 'फाड़ी हुई कविता' एक ऐसे पति की व्यथा-कथा है, जो एक कवि एवं साहित्यकार भी है। 'नया साल' में कुछ भी नया नहीं होता, फिर भी सारी दुनिया किस कदर बाबली हुई रहती है। 'हितैषिणी' शादी जैसी संस्थाओं के पाखण्ड, फ़रेब एवं परम्पराओं से चिपकाव की विद्रूपता पर सशक्त प्रहार करती है। 'छोटे-से शरीर में क़ैदी' शिशुमन की विवशता को चित्रित करती है; वह पूरी तरह माँ-बाप की मूर्खताओं पर निर्भर रहने को विवश है। 'निसर्ग' एक रोमांटिक कहानी है। 'टूट-टूटकर गिरते सितारे' दिखाती है कि कैसे समाज अपने ही शिकंजे में फँसा रहकर ही परेशान होता रहता है!

आर्त-गान (कविता-संग्रह)

'वियोगी होगा पहला कवि, आह से उपजा होगा गान
उमड़कर आँखों से चुपचाप, बही होगी कविता अनजान!'
(सुमित्रा नंदन पंत)
या
'मा निषाद त्वम् गम: प्रतिष्ठाम् शाश्वती समा:
यत् क्रौंच मिथुनादेकम् त्वम् वधी: काम मोहितम्!'
(महर्षि वाल्मीकि)
चाहे तो आदि कवि वाल्मीकि हों, चाहे फिर छायावादी कवि पंत हों, एक बात तो तय है, कि कविता वियोग या विषाद या शोक से उत्सृजित होती है। पहले-पहल की रचनाएँ हैं ये – जीवन के पहले-प्रहर की; अतः बच्चों के उपयुक्त ही हो सकती हैं। बाल-कविता! बाल-कविता इसे मैंने फिर भी इसलिए नहीं कहा है, क्योंकि इनमें मुझे कुछ सार भी सन्निहित लगता रहा है; एकदम तो बकवास नहीं ही हैं ये, जैसी कि बाल (अबोध) -कविता की प्रकृति और प्रवृत्ति होती है। ये कविताएँ 1972 से 1976 के काल-खंड में सृजित हैं; और अभी लगभग अर्ध-

शती की परिपक्व दृष्टि से भी परिमार्जित!

काल-क्रंदन (कविता-संग्रह)

जीवन के प्रथम प्रहर की हृदयाभिव्यक्तियों (1972 से 1976 तक) के 'आर्त-गान' के बाद, 1979 से 1990 तक के द्वादश वर्षीय काल-खण्ड में मैंने जो क्रंदन किया था, उसे मैंने कविता कहा; और उन कविताओं का 'काल-रेख' नाम मैंने चुना था; क्योंकि काल की छाती पर 12 वर्षों तक मैं जो घिसटता रहा था, उस लकीर पीटने को 'काल-रेख' कहना ही मुझे रुच रहा था। परन्तु, कुछ काव्यात्मक स्फुरणा के वश, कुछ काल-अंतराल के प्रभाव-वश मैं अब इसे 'काल-क्रंदन' ही कहना अधिक समीचीन समझ रहा हूँ। साहित्य -- और इसीलिए कविता भी -- जीवन के मूल की अर्थात् सत्य की खोज है: सत्य की परख, यथार्थ की परख! इसमें सब कुछ सुनने-सुनाने, गाने-गवाने ही योग्य है, ऐसा दावा मैं नहीं करता। परन्तु, क्या पढ़ने-पढ़ाने योग्य है, और क्या नहीं, इसका निर्णय भी तो मैं नहीं कर सकता; क्योंकि इसका कण-कण मेरा नितांत निजी सच है! इसमें कितना किस और किसी का भी सच प्रस्तुत है, यह निर्णय उन्हीं पर!

अननुभूत काल (कविता-संग्रह)

अब यह तीसरी काव्य-पुस्तक है! एकदम नवीन काल से सम्बंधित! अभी-अभी हो गुज़रे बड़े मानवीय हादसे को रेखांकित करती हुई: कोरोना की महा-आपदा! विश्व-आपदा! जो न कभी हुई थी, और आशा एवम् प्रार्थना ही कर सकते हैं, न कभी भविष्य में होगी! एकदम नये रूप में दुनिया को सोचने को मजबूर होना पड़ा: 'ऐसा भी हो सकता है?' बेतहाशा भागम-भाग में लगी दुनिया अचानक रुक-सी गयी; नहीं, रुक ही गयी – शब्दशः। वायुयान रुक गये, रेलयान रुक गये, बसें रुक गयीं, सारे वाहन रुक गये। मंदिर, मस्जिद, गुरुद्वारे और चर्च भी बंद हो गये: परमात्मा के घर थे वे! हैं! मक्का, मदीना बंद हो गये। वेटिकन बंद हो गया। वह चिरंतन अटूट आस्था जो रुकने का नाम नहीं लेती थी, और आए-दिन छोटी-छोटी बातों पर सिर-फुटव्वल को बेताब रहती थी, अचानक अपने को सकपकाता हुआ पाने लगी। क्या वह बस आस्था ही भर थी, दुनियावी प्राणियों को भरमाने के लिए; क्या उसमें कोई पारमार्थिक सार न था? तार्किक मन यह सोचने को विवश हो गया।

इस कोरोना-काल ने बहुत सारे पाखण्ड-मण्डन किये हैं!

अम्बेडकर-स्मृति (नाटिका)

जाति की समस्या भारत देश के लिए भयंकर होती जा रही है। यह जाति ही है जिसके चलते भारत-भूमि आक्रांताओं के समक्ष प्रणत हो गयी थी। कड़वी सच्चाई यह है कि राजनीतिक चतुराई के चलते 'सत्ताधीशों' ने अपने आप को 'ऊँचा' और सत्ता से 'वंचित' जनों को 'नीचा' मानना शुरू कर दिया। 'आज़ादी' के अधकचरे प्रयोग के चलते स्थिति और भी भयावह हो गयी है; 'नीचे लोग' ऊँचे लोगों को गरियाते रहते हैं: उसके लिए वे 'मनु-स्मृति' नाम की किसी पौराणिक पुस्तक को गरियाते रहते हैं, जबकि वास्तविकता यह है कि आधुनिक भारत के 99.99 प्रतिशत लोगों ने उस पुस्तक का पढ़ना तो दूर, नाम तक नहीं सुना है। उधर, नये सत्ताधीशों ने नयी स्मृति लिखकर -- संविधान लिखकर (जिसकी ड्राफ्टिंग समिति के अध्यक्ष होने के नाते अम्बेडकर को श्रेय मिला हुआ है) – पूर्ववर्ती समाज-व्यवस्था एवं अर्थ-व्यवस्था को एक सिरे से नकार और नेस्तनाबूद कर दिया है। समाज के बीच इस पर जो बहस चल रही है, उसी का एक छोटा सा नमूना है यह एकांकी!

प्रिय-प्रवास (संकलन, 'हरिऔध' के महाकाव्य का)

'प्रिय-प्रवास' हिंदी -- खड़ी बोली -- का प्रथम महाकाव्य है, जो स्वनाम धन्य महाकवि अयोध्या सिंह उपाध्याय 'हरिऔध' की अमर कृति है। अत्यंत सुमधुर काव्य के रूप में युग-पुरुष श्रीकृष्ण के गोकुल से मथुरा प्रवास और उनके वियोग से व्यथित गोकुल-वासियों की विरह-वेदना का सरस चित्रण इसमें है। वह एक प्रकार से हर प्राणी की वेदना ही है, जो वह उस समय अनुभव करता है जब कोई स्वजन प्रवास हेतु जाता है या प्रयाण करता है, जो कि संसृति का अपरिहार्य लक्षण ही है। आसक्ति, मोह और ममता सब दुःखों का मूल है; जबकि ज्ञान दुःखों से मुक्ति का साधन! इस महा-आख्यान का यही सार अथच् केंद्रीय संदेश समझ में आता है! 'प्रिय-प्रवास' विरह, बिछुड़ने की वेदना, नैसर्गिक प्रेम और विश्व-कल्याण के संदेश का ही महाकाव्यात्मक सरस रूप है। 'विदेह' अरविन्द कुमार ने इस अद्भुत

साहित्यिक कृति को पुनर्संकलित एवं पुनर्मुद्रित करके इसकी एक संक्षिप्त गद्य-कथा भी इसमें प्रस्तुत की है।

प्रार्थना एवं प्राणांश (संकलित प्रेरक काव्यांश)

बहुत ही सरस और सार्थक प्रार्थनाओं एवं प्रेरणादायी काव्यांशों का संचयन है यह! जो न जाने कहाँ-कहाँ से 'विदेह' अरविंद कुमार ने अपनी रुचि अनुकूल संकलित एवं सम्पादित किया है, उन सभी मनीषियों के प्रति हार्दिक आभार व्यक्त करते हुए, जिनकी रचनाएँ और रचनाओं के प्राणांश इसमें संकलित किये गये हैं। जीवन, मृत्यु के वाहन के आगमन की प्रतीक्षा में रत यात्री के कार्य-कलाप और मनोदशा के अतिरिक्त और क्या! इस प्रतीक्षा में क्या-क्या अनहोनी अनुभूतियाँ नहीं होतीं! इस प्रतीक्षा को कम कष्टकर करने के लिए काव्य-शास्त्र अनुश्रवण की अनुशंसा मनीषियों ने की है। साथ ही, प्रार्थना के माहात्म्य को भी स्वीकारा है।

मनो पुब्बंगमा धम्मा, मनो सेट्ठा मनोमया!'

भगवान बुद्ध ने मन से ही सृजित होता हुआ इस सकल प्रपञ्च को बताया है। अत: मन को शुचि एवं निष्कंप रखकर आप संसार का अनुभव बदल सकते हैं। जब सभी कुछ कल्पित है, तो सबको अपना मत अनुभव जैसा ही लगता है। परन्तु, है वस्तुतः सब कुछ कपोल-कल्पित ही: न इसे सत्य कहने का कोई तात्पर्य है, न असत्य कहने का! बस मन को साधने का साधनभर है प्रार्थना!

महामुनि वाल्मीकि रचित् इतिहास : उत्तरकाण्ड (वाल्मीकि के उत्तरकाण्ड का गद्यांतरित सारांश)

'रामायण' आदिकाव्य है, न केवल भारतवर्ष का, अपितु सकल मानव-समाज का भी। महर्षि वाल्मीकि-कृत यह काव्य-पुस्तक वस्तुतः तत्कालीन इतिहास है: उस राजवंश का, जिसकी कीर्ति हज़ारों वर्ष पश्चात् भी आज तक अक्षुण्ण है। उस राजवंश के तत्कालीन यशस्वी सम्राट 'राम' का इसमें वर्णन है। राम-राज्य की व्यवस्था, जिसका वर्णन ऋषि ने किया है, आज भी शासन-व्यवस्था के हेतु आदर्श मानी जाती है।

लेखक ने संस्कृत के ग्रंथ का मात्र सार रूप यहाँ प्रस्तुत किया है; सब प्रकार की काव्यात्मकता और अतिशयोक्तियों का निवारण करते हुए। साथ ही, आलंकारिकता को आधुनिक संदर्भों से जोड़ते हुए

ऐतिहासिक-वैज्ञानिक अर्थों में भी विषय को समझाने का प्रयास किया है।

कितना यह किसको भाता है, यह तो हर व्यक्ति की अपनी-अपनी रुचि और सोच पर निर्भर करेगा; बहरहाल, लेखक ने अपना दृष्टिकोण प्रस्तुत किया है, वह भी इस चिन्ता से कि नयी पीढ़ी अपनी बहुमूल्य विरासत – गौरवशाली इतिहास -- की ओर

लेखक-परिचय

'विदेह' अरविन्द कुमार

भारतीय साहित्य की उदात्त पीठिका को आधुनिक संदर्भों से संपृक्त करने वाले सारस्वत साधक एवं विशिष्ट लेखन-शैली के प्रणेता वरिष्ठ साहित्यकार श्री अरविन्द कुमार 'विदेह' का जन्म 6 अप्रैल 1957 ई को उत्तर प्रदेश के गौतमबुद्धनगर जनपद की जेवर तहसील के छोटे-से गाँव 'मारहरा' में हुआ था। आपके माता-पिता की मानव-मूल्यों में गहरी आस्था रही है। सीमित संसाधनों, बल्कि विपन्नता, के बावजूद भी आप सफलता के लाभी हुए। आपने तत्कालीन आगरा विश्वविद्यालय के अलीगढ़ स्थित धर्मसमाज कॉलेज से भौतिक विज्ञान में स्नातकोत्तर उपाधि प्राप्त की है। आप देश के प्रतिष्ठित बैंक – भारतीय स्टेट बैंक – में दीर्घकालीन सेवा प्रदान करने के उपरांत दिसम्बर, 2018 में सहायक महाप्रबंधक के पद से सेवा निवृत्त हुए हैं।

श्री 'विदेह' छात्र-जीवन से ही अत्यंत मेधावी रहे हैं। विज्ञान-संवर्ग के विद्यार्थी होते हुए भी आपकी साहित्य के प्रति गहरी अभिरुचि रही है। साहित्य के प्रति आपका अनुराग इतना प्रबल रहा है कि बैंकिंग सेक्टर में अति व्यस्त जीवन-शैली वाली नौकरी करते हुए भी आप साहित्य और लेखन से अनवरत रूप से जुड़े रहे हैं। उनकी रचनाएँ तत्कालीन 'कादम्बिनी' जैसी लब्ध-प्रतिष्ठ पत्रिकाओं में काफ़ी पहले छप चुकी हैं; और उनके

एकदम ध्यान नहीं दे रही है। उसका एक कारण ग्रंथों का संस्कृत में होना, और दूसरा अत्यधिक प्रतीकात्मक होने के कारण कपोल-कल्पित-सा लगना, भी हो सकता है; उसी कारण का निवारण करने का यह विनीत प्रयास है।

XXX

अन्य लेख एवं कविताएँ अन्य हिंदी, अंग्रेज़ी पत्र-पत्रिकाओं में यदा-कदा छपते रहे हैं। साथ ही, आपने हिंदी एवं अंग्रेजी भाषा के साहित्य का विशद अध्ययन एवं सृजन किया है। संस्कृत एवं पाली भाषा के साहित्य में भी आपकी गहरी अभिरुचि है।

विभिन्न विधाओं में आपने अब तक 27 ग्रंथों का प्रणयन किया है, जिनमें 17 अंग्रेजी एवं 10 हिंदी भाषा में हैं। हिंदी की पुस्तकों में 03 कहानी-संग्रह (अनपढ़ लिपि, पाषाण युग, निसर्ग); 03 कविता-संग्रह (आर्त-गान, काल-क्रन्दन, अननुभूत काल); 01 नाटिका (अम्बेडकर-स्मृति); 01 काव्य-संचयन (प्रार्थना एवं प्राणांश) उल्लेखनीय हैं। इसके अतिरिक्त आपने खड़ी बोली के प्रथम महाकाव्य 'प्रिय-प्रवास' को भी पुनर्संकलित एवं पुनर्मुद्रित किया है; तथा साथ ही, वाल्मीकि रामायण के उत्तरकाण्ड का गद्यांतरण इतिहास के दृष्टिकोण से आपने 'महामुनि वाल्मीकि रचित् इतिहास: रामायण – उत्तरकाण्ड' नामक पुस्तक के रूप में किया है।

अंग्रेजी भाषा में आपकी उपन्यास श्रृंखला 'Hypocrisy & Reality' है जिसके अब तक 9 खण्ड वह प्रस्तुत कर चुके हैं (Beyond the Pale; Wilderness of Literacy; Advent of Time; Devoid of Shelter; Price of Refuge; Hatred towards Love; Towards the *Yoga*; On the Descent; In the Exile)। इसके अतिरिक्त, 01 Comedietta (*Chambellion*); 01 Short Story collection (Brainy Beasts); 01 Poetry anthology (Bewailing Muse); 01 Drama (Self-styled Sovereign, the Judiciary); पौराणिक ग्रंथ 'शिव-पुराण' के आधुनिक संदर्भों में अध्ययन पर आधारित 01 पुस्तक (Procreation, the Adorable); 2017 के साहित्य नोबेल पुरस्कार विजेता, Kazuo Ishiguro, के प्रथम उपन्यास 'A

Pale View of the Hills' पर आधारित 01 समीक्षात्मक ग्रंथ (Nagasaki: Bomb & Aftermath) हैं।

'विदेह' जितने मौलिक सर्जक हैं उतने ही समर्थ अनुवादक भी हैं। उन्होंने हिंदी के 02 काव्य-संग्रहों – 'निर्विकार' मुकेश के 'हत्यारी सदी में जीवन की खोज', और 'अश्वघोष' ओमप्रकाश शर्मा के 'अदृश्य का यथार्थ' – का काव्यात्मक अनुवाद अंग्रेजी में किया है, जो क्रमश: 'Search for Life' एवं 'Reality of Invisible' के नाम से प्रकाशित हुई हैं।

'विदेह' के व्यक्तित्व का निर्माण घोर विपन्नता और कठोर संघर्षों ने किया है, जिसका प्रभाव उनकी लेखन-शैली पर निर्भीक अभिव्यक्ति और बेवाकी के रूप में देखा जा सकता है। आपके जीवन का अनुभव अत्यन्त व्यापक रहा है। आपने विपन्नता भी भोगी है, और सुख-सुविधा-सम्पन्न अमेरिकी जीवन भी जीया है; साथ ही, अनेक विदेश-यात्राओं का भी आपको अनुभव है।

केवल साहित्य ही नहीं, 'विदेह' की प्रवृत्तियों में ध्यान-साधना, विपश्यना, योग-साधना, प्राकृतिक-जीवन, आरोग्य, शाकाहार, बागवानी, पर्यटन और पैदल भ्रमण भी सम्मिलित हैं।

2024 के हिंदी दिवस पर – 14 सितंबर को – 'विदेह' को 'शुभम् साहित्य, कला एवम् संस्कृति संस्थान' द्वारा उनके सर्वोच्च सम्मान 'शुभम् रत्न' से सम्मानित किया गया।

'विदेह' की पुस्तकें 'Notion Press', Blue Rose One, Amazon और Flipkart पर तीनों ही प्रारूपों – ebooks, paperback एवम् hard cover – में उपलब्ध हैं।

XXX

About the Author

'Videh' Arvind Kumar

An unflinching adorer of the goddess of wisdom, the *Saraswatee*, and the one who has associated the lofty traditions of Indian literature with the present day contexts, and also, an author of an uncanny style of his own, the seasoned litterateur, *'Videh' Arvind Kumar,* was born on 6th of April, 1957, at a hamlet called *'Maar-Haraa'* in *Jewar Tehseel* of *Gautam Buddha Nagar* distt. in UP. His parents were staunch votaries of human values. Despite unbearable financial constraints, rather extreme wretchedness, he overcame the hurdles of existence and succeeded. He is a post-graduate in Physics from D S College, *Aleegarh*, affiliated to the then *Aagaraa* University. He retired as an Asstt General Manager from the esteemed Bank – State Bank of India – after putting in a long as well as illustrious service there.

'Videh' has been meritorious ever since his school days. Despite being a science stream scholar, he has been showing a keen interest in literature all along. His bonding with literature has been so strong that notwithstanding his pursuing such a busy job as Banking, he managed to sustain his love for literature. His works have been published decades back in the then esteemed magazines such as *'Kaadambinee'*. Also, his stray articles and compositions have found place in various magazines and journals now and then. Besides, he has been a voracious reader of literature and other stuff both in *Hindee* and English languages, apart from himself being a prolific writer and a poet. He is also an adorer of the literature in *Sanskrit* and

Pali languages.

In variegated genre he has composed as many as 27 books so far, of which, 17 are in English and 10 in *Hindee*. Among the *Hindee* books, there are 03 story anthologies (*Anapadh Lipi; Paashaan Yug; Nisarg*); 03 poetry anthologies (*Aaart Gaan; Kaal Krandan; Ananubhoot Kaal*); 01 drama (*Ambedkar Smriti*); 01 collection of select poetic pieces (*Praarthanaa evam Praanaansh*). Aside of this, he has compiled, commented, edited and got re-published the first epic of the *Khadee Bolee Hindee*, the *Priya Pravaas*; and a book entitled *'Mahaamuni Vaalmeeki Rachit Itihaas: Raamaayan -- Uttar Kaand'* which presents, in succinct prose form, the ancient history of India as narrated in the most ancient epic.

As regards English oeuvre of *'Videh'*, he has so far published 9 volumes of the long fiction series 'Hypocrisy & Reality' (Beyond the Pale; Wilderness of Literacy; Advent of Time; Devoid of Shelter; Price of Refuge; Hatred towards Love; Towards the *Yoga*; On the Descent; In the Exile) with yet more planned to come. Besides, 01 Comedietta (*Chambellion*); 01 Short Story collection (Brainy Beasts); 01 Poetry anthology (Bewailing Muse); 01 Drama (Self-Styled Sovereign, the Judiciary); 01 book based on the study of mythological volume '*Shiva Puraan*' in the present day context (Procreation, the Adorable); 01 commentary book on the first novel – 'A Pale View of the Hills' -- of the 2017 Nobel Literature laureate, Kazuo Ishiguro (Nagasaki: Bomb & Aftermath) are other books.

Not only an original writer as well as thinker, but also, a capable and versatile translator is *'Videh'* inasmuch as he has translated in English free verse form 02 *Hindee* poetry anthologies, viz. *'Hatyaaree Sadee Mein Jeevan Kee Khoj'* of *'Nirvikaar'* Mukesh Kumaar, and *'Adrishya Kaa Yathaarth'* of *'Ashwaghosh'* Omprakaash Sharmaa with the titles of the books being *seriatim* as 'Search for Life' and 'Reality of Invisible'.

The persona of *'Videh'* has been moulded by constant struggles and abject adversities, which have metamorphosed into his style of narration being quite frank as well as bland, if only straightforward.

His experiences of life are multifarious. He has not only suffered the pangs of extreme poverty and adversity in his childhood, but also, enjoyed the comforts and pleasures of the modern world by living in America. Besides, he has visited and toured in various foreign countries, too.

Not only in literature, but also, in exotic pursuits like meditation, spiritual practice, *Vipashyanaa, Yoga* practice, naturopathy, natural living, *Aarogya*, vegetarianism, gardening, tourism and long walks on foot *'Videh'* is equally active.

To add to his laurels, *'Videh'* has been honoured with their highest honour *'Shubham Ratna'* by the institution *'Shubham Saahitya, Kalaa Evam Sanskriti Sansthaan'* on the occasion of *Hindee Divas*, i.e. on 14th September, 2024.

The books of *'Videh'* are available in all the three formats, viz. eBooks, paperbacks and hardcovers from the Notion Press, Blue Rose One, Amazon and the Flipkart.

XXX

www.ingramcontent.com/pod-product-compliance
Lightning Source LLC
Chambersburg PA
CBHW021232130726
47988CB00002B/931